A LIFE WORTH LIVING

A Novel by T. L. SCOTT

08 AUGUST 2010 to 23 November, 2014

This book is a work of fiction. Names, characters, places and incidents either are products of the author's imagination or are used fictitiously. Any resemblance to actual events or locales or persons, living or dead is entirely coincidental.

A Life Worth Living

This book is dedicated to my children. You show me with ease how to embrace life. I hope you never forget to embrace the simple joys in life and always love unconditionally. Most of all, may you never lose your curiosity and remember to always look for the good in all things.

A special thank you to all the patient and understanding people that provided feedback during the development of the story. It will always be appreciated.

Cover art design by Digital Donna. Your gifts touched so many. I am forever grateful.

A very special thank you to Bronwyn, my editor. Your insight and perspective along with your persistence and patience made this revision possible.

Chapter 1

The light from the computer washed the color from his face. It was impossible to tell how much the dark circles under his eyes were caused by the shadows and how much by fatigue. He was sitting forward in his ergonomic leather chair, his nose only eighteen inches from the screen. His features were slack. The overall look was that of an exhausted corporate executive.

On a distant level, he'd registered that the sun had set hours ago. He filed that information away as important but not immediately relevant.

His coffee cup sat on the coaster his daughter had made for him in her second-grade art class. The beverage had gone cold hours ago. This, along with many other things, he wasn't aware of. He was so engrossed in his work that everything else had faded into the background.

He scrolled on the mouse with his left hand while his right, seemingly of its own volition, entered numbers into the adding machine. The seemingly endless loop of paper cascaded off the desk and lay coiled in a mass on the floor. Its length a literal measurement of how long he'd been at his task.

This ability to block out the distractions around him, and focus on the task at hand, was one of the things that made him so good at his job. But, as with all things, a balance must be maintained. Dave was not balanced. He was focused. Focused on his job.

The shrill ring of his desk phone brought him back to the here and now. He glanced at the clock above his door and was surprised to see how late it was. Everyone else had left for the night, and here he was, yet again, still working.

He picked up the phone and leaned back in his chair. He rubbed his tired eyes with one hand. "Thompson here," he said.

"Do you have any idea what time it is?" Debbie immediately asked.

"Yes Debbie, I just looked at the clock and I—"

"Don't tell me," she said cutting him off. "You lost track of time again, right?"

"You didn't realize that it's already past eight? Sometimes, Dave, I feel like you prefer spending your time at the office instead of with me!"

"You know what?" She paused and took a calming breath. "I don't even care anymore." There was a tiredness in her voice that hadn't been there until recently.

"Debbie, calm down a minute, I'm in the office working. It's not like I'm out at a bar or something. I'm working hard here!" He said with heat in his voice.

"Dave, don't you get it? You are still deciding to spend time doing something other than being here with us."

"Do you think I like working so many hours? I want to be home. I'd love to be able to kick my feet up and watch a movie. Instead, I'm here, wracking my brains."

"Don't you dare talk like you're the only one that works around here! I put in damn long hours too! The difference is that I at least try to work my schedule around our kids' big events. Speaking of which, while you've been *wracking your brains*, Aidan scored the only goal of the game. You not only weren't there to see him do it, yet again, you weren't even home for dinner, so he could share it with you then!"

Dave didn't have anything to say to that, and the silence hung heavy over the line.

"Do you want to know what he said about that, Dave? He said I should go easy on you because you were working hard for all of us. Do you get that? He was defending *you* for not being there for *him*." Debbie had dropped her voice and was speaking slowly, enunciating each word.

He knew from long experience that she only did it when she was really upset about something, like now, for example.

"We have great kids, and you don't spend nearly enough time with them, and you know it! I already put your dinner in the fridge for whenever you decide to come home."

Dave looked at the phone in his hand.

"She hung up on me?"

He could still hear the echo of the click as the line had gone dead. He shook his head and put the phone down. As upset as he was about the conversation, he had to admit that everything she had said was true. They both knew it too. He leaned back and let out a long, tired breath, and rubbed his eyes some more.

This conversation had been played out many times, in many different ways, over the years. He wanted to be with his kids more. Of course, he knew how great they were. Both Aidan and Summer deserved better from him. He really wished he could get it all done and have the time to spend with them. He knew that they had been blessed with two great kids. He was torn. He worked so hard to provide for his family. All he really wanted was for them to have the best life possible. These long hours were for them, not for his ego. He just wanted to do the right thing. To be honest, this problem had only gotten worse over the years.

His eyes focused on the picture that sat on the corner of his desk. It'd been taken how long ago? Was it possible that three years had already gone by?

Aidan and Summer were on each side of Debbie, and they were all making funny faces. The picture had been taken on the dock behind her parents' vacation house on the lake. It had been a great vacation. That was the reason it was on the desk. No matter how bad the day was, seeing his family always brought a smile to his face. It did so this time as well.

At the other end of that broken line, Debbie was trying to get herself under control. After hanging up the phone, she sagged back against the doorframe and slowly collapsed onto the kitchen floor. The kids were up in their rooms, so she didn't think they'd heard the heated exchange. She was so tired; mentally and emotionally exhausted. She sat there, with her arms wrapped around her knees and her head resting against the solid wood of the door frame, her eyes tightly closed. There was such a weight pushing down on her. She didn't feel like she had the strength left in her to get back up again.

"Why does he do this?" She asked herself for what seemed like the thousandth time. She didn't really believe that he was cheating on her. But that was what it *felt* like. He was choosing to spend his time at work instead of home with her. The job was his mistress, and she was damn tired of it.

A tear leaked out from her closed eyelid. She angrily wiped it away and took a couple of deep breaths.

Footsteps pounded down the back stairs.

Debbie picked herself up off the floor. She wouldn't let her kids see her like this.

"Hi Mom," said Summer as she walked to the fridge.

"No ice cream at this time of night, young lady. You know the rules," Debbie said without turning around. She was surprised by how normal her voice sounded. Inside she felt like everything was coming apart. Her hands were shaking. It was a good thing she had them busy rinsing off the dinner plates.

"I know, Mom. I'm just getting a glass of milk … Mom, are you okay?"

"Yeah, honey. Why?" Asked Debbie as she turned to look at her daughter.

"You just looked, I don't know, upset there for a minute."

"Everything's okay, sweetie. Is your homework done? It's almost time for bed." Debbie was reminded just how perceptive her little girl was. She'd been that way since she was very young.

"Yeah, I really just came down to give you a goodnight kiss."

Debbie finished loading the dishwasher then followed Summer up to her room. She spent a few minutes talking with her daughter before tucking her in for the night. They had their routine. Summer still liked to have the covers tucked in tight on both sides. Once she was snugly tucked in, almost swaddled, Debbie would kiss her on the forehead, both cheeks, her chin, and then a quick peck on the nose. Then she would touch her forehead to her daughter's.

"Sweet dreams, baby girl."

"You too, Mom. Love you," Summer answered. By the time Debbie put her hand on the doorknob, her little girl was already drifting off.

Debbie walked down the carpeted hall and knocked on Aidan's door. She hoped he wasn't still playing his video games. He was good about following the rule of homework first, but not so good about stopping his game to go to bed on time.

After she was done following the same routine with Aidan, she made the long walk down the hall, to her empty bedroom. It was times like this that she felt so terribly lonely. She hated going to bed alone. It always felt too big, and no matter how many blankets she had it felt cold.

She'd spent enough nights alone when Dave was in the Navy. That was different though. He was away from her for a good reason; he was serving his country. Even though she hated being alone then, she understood why. Lately, her well of understanding was running dry.

Back at the office, Dave was still working away. He looked over the spreadsheet that had held his attention for the better part of the last twelve hours and wondered, yet again, where things had gone so wrong.

The economy couldn't account for the negative yield by itself. What was behind the dip? He hoped the trend he felt that he was onto wasn't real. Something did not add up. When that had happened in the past, it was because someone had tried to cover something up. He really hoped that was not the case here.

Bob had been with the company for as long as he had. He knew his family. The kids had played Frisbee together at the company picnic last year. Dave hoped there were other reasons for the disparities he was seeing. Oh well, that was a knot to keep worrying at tomorrow. He put all the pages back into the file and tossed the Styrofoam container that held the remnants of his meatball sub into the trash can. He took a minute and looked around his office to make sure that he didn't forget anything.

Fortunately, at this hour, traffic was light, and he pulled into his garage twenty minutes later, closing the door to the garage he looked at the digital clock on the oven as it changed to 11:27. *Damn, I didn't think it was that late*, he said to himself as he put his keys on the hook by the door.

He didn't have an appetite for leftovers and decided to quietly make his way up to bed. Before he reached the stairs, he noticed the pillow and blanket on the couch. He just stood there staring at them for a minute. The message could not have been any clearer.

Chapter 2

Dave woke up at six, as usual, happy to discover that there was a distinct advantage to waking up in the guest room. His senses were drawn to the sounds and smell of percolating coffee. He stood up from the bed and stretched. He was awarded a rapid staccato popping from his abused back. *I need to get a better mattress for that bed,* he thought.

He bent down and tried to touch his toes, falling well short of his mark he stayed that way until he felt his muscles loosen up. He only got marginally closer to reaching the floor. Slowly he stood up, his eyes settled on the sight of the twisted mess of sheets and blanket. It was clear that he had not had peaceful dreams.

Dave wasn't surprised to find that Debbie had thought ahead and put his clothes for the day in the downstairs bathroom. One of the things he had always loved about her was the way that she planned well in advance.

Stepping out of the bathroom, he said to himself, *Okay, it is a new day that is full of possibilities*. He followed the tantalizing aroma of caffeine goodness into the kitchen and busied himself with making breakfast.

Debbie came into the kitchen as he was finishing up the batter for the pancakes. She poured herself a cup of coffee and refreshed his mug as well.

"Let's talk before the kids come down," she said without preamble.

Dave took his seat expecting to hear all about how he had come home late. They both knew these dance steps well. To his surprise, she didn't question where he had been. She came right to the point.

"Dave, I'm tired of you working so many hours. Please, don't say anything just yet," Debbie said, holding up her hand for him to stop.

He obliged and shut his half-open mouth.

"Hear me out, okay? I know, I work long hours too. The difference is, mine is shift work and scheduled. You are working all this overtime, all of the time, and for what? You're on salary, Dave. They don't pay you overtime."

"You're right," he said in a reasonable tone of voice, "but one of the expectations is that longer hours are worked by those on salary. That's why we are on salary."

"I know, but you know as well as I do that no one works the kinds of hours that you do. It has to stop, Dave. You have to cut back and start focusing some of that energy back on your family."

"Debbie, that's a cheap shot. You know the reason I work so hard is *for* this family."

"I used to think so. Now I'm not so sure. I'm starting to think that you need to believe that you are the one that gives the most. There are other ways of giving, Dave."

"I know. I'll work on scaling back."

She looked at him for a while before responding. "I really hope so. The kids need you around more. *I* need you around more. I miss the way we used to be. This weekend is going to be a good break for all of us."

He couldn't hide his confusion. Fortunately, he knew better than to say anything.

"You have got to be kidding me!" She couldn't help raising her voice. "You actually forgot that we're going to my parents this weekend, haven't you?"

There was no point in denying it.

"This is just so damn typical of you lately! All you have on your mind is what's going on at the office. You're oblivious to what's happening here! Listen to me, we are going this weekend, so you do whatever you need to do to make it happen." She waved her arms to the side expansively.

"I will not tell my parents that we're not coming. They're looking forward to spending time with all of us. Dad's really looking forward to going out in the boat fishing with the boys. Don't ruin this."

She would have said more, but Aidan walked in, rubbing the sleep from his eyes.

"Hey, Mom," he said before kissing her on the cheek. "You are up kind'a early. Dad, you're making pancakes? Can we have bacon too?"

"Sure, son. Can you get it out of the fridge for me?"

They fell into the comforting routine of breakfast. Summer was excited to find out that they were having pancakes. Dave, knowing that she would be the last one to sit down, had made the final two pancakes special for her.

"Dad, you know I'm not a baby, anymore right?" she complained in her ever-so-mature thirteen-year-old voice. "I don't even like Mickey Mouse."

Dave watched her put the face on Mickey with the syrup, in-spite-of her protests. He couldn't help but smile a little.

"I'll remember the next time, sweetie." They both knew he wouldn't. They also knew she would have been a little disappointed if he stopped doing it.

The kids put their dishes in the sink and went to their rooms to finish getting ready for school. Dave took advantage of the moment of privacy to put his arms around his wife as she was rinsing off the dishes. They both just stood there like that for a couple of minutes. She moved her hands up to caress his arms, as he nuzzled her ear.

They broke their embrace as the kids thundered down the steps. Debbie caught his hand before he walked away.

"Dave, please don't be late tonight."

"I won't, honey." He put his other arm around her and gave her a long kiss.

"Come on, Dad," called Summer. "We're going to be late."

"I love you, honey," Dave said to his wife.

"I know you do. I love you too. Now go, before the kids are late for school."

Chapter 3

"Good morning, Mr. Thompson."

"Oh, I'm sorry, Rosie. Good morning to you too. How's the family? Is Billy sleeping through the night yet?"

"He's getting better. Monday he only woke up once and went back down right after he ate. Last night was not so good, but I'm hoping tonight will be better."

"I'm sure it will be. Have a good day."

"See you later Mr. Thompson."

As soon as Dave opened the door to his office, the phone started ringing.

He quickly took the three steps across the carpeted floor to his desk and said, "Thompson here."

"Hi Dave, I know you're just getting in, but could you grab the Klase file and come to my office?"

"Of course, Jim, what's the angle?"

"No worries, we'll look it over together and see if there's anything to it, when you get here."

"Okay boss, see you in a minute." Dave hung up the phone and went to get the file. He went over the case in his mind. He didn't like talking about any file without having it fresh in his mind. He paused at the door before leaving his office and made sure that everything was locked up. He hadn't even had the time to boot up his computer, so that was one less step to worry about. All that was left was locking the door. Keys, where are the keys? He checked his pockets without success. Then he checked his coat pocket. Not there either. Starting to feel frantic he spotted them sitting in the saucer on his desk, as usual.

Dave made his way down the hall with his focus on the open file in his hands. He almost took out two people on his way and would have, if not for the other people's quick reflexes. He made his half-hearted apologies and continued on his way.

By the time Dave left Jim's office three hours had passed, and he had a new case to look into. Another case! *I have too much to do now and not enough time to get it done. Well, it sounds like more long hours.*

Dave leaned back and closed his eyes for a minute. When he felt that he had calmed back down, he sat forward and opened his eyes, they settled on the picture sitting on the corner of his desk. Right there was the reason why he did what he did. The reason he worked himself so hard was his family. As usual, Debbie was right. He was missing out on too much of their lives. Plus, he had made a promise to her, and he intended to keep it. He was going to scale back his hours. A smile crept onto his face as he thought of going fishing with his father-in-law. It *had* been too long since he had done something fun. Maybe this weekend would even help to bring him and Debbie closer together again.

They'd been drifting apart for a while now. That was normal, right? They had been married for 18 years. It was normal for the passion to fade. As soon as he thought that, he knew he was deluding himself. It was more serious than that. They'd been growing apart, and he knew he was to blame. He had focused so much on work that he had disengaged from the family.

He had disengaged from Debbie. *When was the last time we went out without the kids? When was the last time I brought her flowers?*

The truth was, he had become so busy with work that it was pretty much all he thought about. When he wasn't at work, he was thinking about what he needed to do when he got back to work. Everything else was kind of on autopilot. It all faded into the background while he focused on work.

My family has faded into the background.

That's not who I want to be. They deserve better from me.

Dave opened up the Klase file and began to dig into the discrepancies.

Two hours later his train of thought was derailed. An important client, Karl Williams arrived, and he had to take care of him.

The meeting lasted longer than Dave wanted. That was another problem with being thorough, it usually led to delving deeper into issues and taking up more time than expected. In the end, though, the results were complete and rarely required re-work.

Dave looked at the clock on the wall and made a plan for what he wanted to get done with the little time remaining of the workday.

Tonight, you have to get home at a decent hour, he told himself.

He went to his coffee pot and topped off his cup with some liquid alertness, to help power through the afternoon doll-drums.

Most people looked at the field of accounting with as much enthusiasm as a trip to the dentist. Dave still found it to be a fascinating job, and at times, even exciting. For example, the work he was doing now, going back and analyzing the transactions in Bob's department, was interesting because it provided a sense of mystery.

He was like a detective trying to figure out how to solve the case. Okay, that was being a bit dramatic, but it was fun figuring out what actually happened. Occasionally, it even led to criminal charges, when people thought they could get away with fraud or embezzlement.

Even if the infraction wasn't criminal, they were punished by a fate that was likely as painful. They were fired and "somehow" the word spread around the major players what had happened, so their professional lives died a quick and very painful death.

God, he hoped Bob wasn't that stupid!

Dave told himself for the thousandth time that it was not his problem. He wasn't the one that decided to step across the line. He was one of the good guys. It was because of him and his department that the company was able to stop the hemorrhage those thieves caused in the financial flow which was the company's life blood.

Wow, he just realized that he had already become convinced that Bob was guilty. He hadn't found the smoking gun yet, but Dave knew that when everything was put together, it would be clear that Bob had tried to cover his tracks. Now, all he needed to do was to pull it all together and present his findings to Jim. The day just got a bit brighter for Dave. Bob's future, on the other hand, had just taken a steep curve in the road. Of course, he didn't know it yet.

The next time he looked at the clock it was 6:15. *Okay, not bad, still a decent time to call it a day.* He felt good about himself. He had made some real progress on the cases he was working on and was leaving the office at a decent time for the first time in way too long.

The drive home was flowing smoothly. As usual, Dave used the time to go over his day at work and think of what he would need to do once he returned.

The traffic slowed as he approached the next intersection. In the distance, he saw flashing blue lights on the trees. The rubber-neckers were slowing traffic. *Why can't they just focus on driving?* He knew the answer was that people had an inherent morbid curiosity. Unfortunately, his understanding of human nature did not help the snarled traffic move along any better.

When he finally made it to the intersection, he succumbed to his own morbid curiosity. He saw the flashing blue lights of the emergency vehicles casting shadows on the crumpled bodies of the Honda and the Cadillac where they had met each other in the middle of the crossroad. Judging by the three ambulances on the scene, it was going to be a terrible night for some of them.

It was a fact of life that things could change in the blink of an eye. Those people were just going about their business, when suddenly, everything changed.

Dave realized that he did not want to risk leaving Debbie the way things were between them. *I love her, and she deserves better from me. They all deserve better from me.*

With a renewed sense of commitment, Dave continued on his way home. He sent up a silent prayer for those involved in the accident.

Chapter 4

Dave walked into the house and was met with the sound of the TV coming from the family room, and a bass beat throbbing from one of the upstairs bedrooms. He knew that would be Summer listening to her current favorite group. He knew it wasn't Aidan because he preferred to listen to his music on his headphones.

He hung his coat up in the closet off the foyer and set his satchel down in its usual spot and kicked his shoes off. He walked down the hallway to the family room. He stood behind the couch and bent down to kiss Debbie on the back of the neck. She startled a little at his touch. At thirty-nine she was still the most beautiful woman he knew. He often wondered what she ever saw in him. Not that he asked that question out loud or too often unless she started to wonder the same thing. Lately, he feared she had been asking herself that very question.

It's not that she was doing anything differently, really, there just seemed to be a kind of coolness settling in between them. Where before there had been a burning desire, now there was a softly glowing ember. That would be normal and even welcome except that they were not reaching for each other anymore. The little things are what make a marriage strong. Little things like a touch while passing, reaching across the table over breakfast while making a point, the simple desire to touch each other, to be *in* touch with each other. That desire seemed to have gone into a hiatus. He still held out the hope that it was only a temporary pause.

The empty bottle of Pinot Grigio on the table and the nearly empty glass in her beautiful hand told him that she was really upset.

He sat down next to her on the brown leather couch, looked at her and said, "I'm sorry."

She knew him too well. Raising an eyebrow, she asked, "what is it that you are sorry about?"

He decided to plunge right in and get to the truth at the very heart of the matter, at least in his opinion.

"I'm sorry that I'm not here more for you and the kids."

Debbie looked him right in the eye and surprised him with her response. "Forget about me, Dave! The kids are getting older fast, and you are missing out on things. These are things that you cannot get back! As much as they say they understand, it still hurts them when they can't share these things with their Dad. Listen, I know that you didn't have a Dad that you could lean on, but these kids do! It's just that you are so busy at work that you are not there for them. Don't get me wrong, you are providing for them very well financially and materially. That's great! But they need more from you. They need *you*! Okay, don't forget about me because I need you too! Damn it, you need to do something about working all this extra time! Nobody else does it. Why do you need to?"

Well ...? He thought, looking at his wife. *Why do I need to? I have good people working for me that know what they are doing. Why am I the one that always stays late and comes in early? Ok, part of it, to be honest, is because it's what I have always done. It's a habit I have fallen into. But the question is: Do I NEED to do it? I need to really look at this from a different perspective.*

"Once the audit is done, and I am ready for the meeting, and things settle down again."

"No, No, NO! That's just a stalling tactic."

"Debbie, I told you this morning that I would start pulling back. I have been thinking about it, and I really do need to stop working so many hours. Pick your chin up, honey. I admit it for the record: You Were Right." He said with a big smile on his face. "Hey look, I'm here, and it isn't that late.

"Dave, you do realize that it's already past 7, right?"

"Well, it isn't *that* late," he said with a half-smile.

Debbie felt a glimmer of something she hadn't felt in a long time. Dave had been pulling away for so long it was hard to believe that he would actually follow through and put more focus on the family.

Dave had been watching her face carefully, and he saw the brief flicker of hope fade away as quickly as it had appeared. He couldn't blame her. He had made promises like this before only to have the same old pattern re-emerge in short order.

He didn't like seeing the look of doubt cloud her beautiful face. He promised her in his heart that he would follow through this time. For some reason, he felt that this time it was more important than ever before.

With that settled, at least for now, they settled into a comfortable night together. He poured them each what remained of the Pinot Grigio and then followed her lead as they went through the routine of making dinner. They had always worked well as a team and cooking together was something they both really enjoyed. Meanwhile, upstairs, Summer continued to enjoy whatever new music group she was into, and Aidan likely was either reading or studying.

After dinner, Debbie took up her place on the couch with her feet tucked under her still attractive posterior. Dave always loved the way she curled up like a cat. She had no idea how attractive she was just sitting there like that. Lately, it seemed that it was the only time that she looked like she was relaxed. She really looked like the girl that he fell in love with back in school.

The kids stayed up with them until, after the usual amount of protests, they went off to bed. Dave moved over to the couch to sit next to Debbie. She stretched out her long legs and put them on his lap. They stayed that way while the nightly news doled out the latest drama. The economy was terrible. Politicians, as usual, were blaming each other very eloquently while seeming to completely miss the point that it was their job to work together to fix these problems. News-bites of murder and mayhem on a worldwide scale did not make for a good way to end the day, but as the headline said, it was the nightly news. After that dose of what passed for their current reality, they both needed a laugh, so they turned on a late-night talk show. Even there they heard about the headlines, albeit delivered in a comedic fashion. The comedy helped Dave feel a little better about his lot in life. He was better off than a lot of other people. He realized that all that could change for him too. He had a clear vision of the flashing blue lights of the emergency vehicles lighting up the dark. Life was short, and he was even more convinced that his decision to focus on spending more time with his family was the right choice. He needed to work on his relationship with Debbie too.

The distance they had grown away from each other was something that he was very uncomfortable with. The sad thing was that he knew he was at fault. She had made strides to keep their relationship interesting. They still enjoyed a date night, even if it had gone from once a week to once a month or so. They were both so busy. Even so, he knew they had been drifting apart for a long while and vowed to do something about it this time.

As they settled into bed, he had hopes of them coming closer together. He was surprised at how much he craved her touch right then. He knew it was not to be when she reached up and turned off her light then turned her back to him. He contented himself with reading up on the Wall Street Journal. Not exactly dull, but not the scintillating night he had fantasized about while sitting on the couch.

He put the magazine down and realized he was not working on bridging the gap that separated them. He put away the Journal, turned off the light, and rolled toward her. He gently stroked the hair off her shoulder. "I miss you, Debbie."

Debbie had been lying there just thinking about how there should be more passion. Well, maybe not passion, but at least some desire left. She tried to make the feeling come, but she was tired of being the one to try to make things right. She was just so tired.

When she felt Dave's hand tentatively touch her shoulder, she felt a spark ignite. Sure, it was a little spark, but it was something. She rolled over to him and put her hand on his cheek. They lay there, just looking into each other's eyes for a while. There was just enough light coming in through the window for her to make out his face. They were both hesitant about how to go from there. It had been a long time since they had been intimate.

Dave was surprised she had turned toward him and was afraid of doing anything that would ruin this moment. He was not thinking beyond the moment. He was afraid to. He thought about doing a hundred things to move beyond this moment. He didn't so much as flinch a finger, afraid to push is luck. He was surprised to realize that he was holding his breath. He was happy that she had turned to him instead of rejecting his clumsy advance. He didn't want to push her away, but he knew that if he didn't do something, she would turn away from him again.

His other hand reached out to hers, and they clasped their fingers together. He leaned forward and put his forehead to hers. He could hear her soft breathing in the darkened room.

Debbie realized that the spark had started a smoldering heat inside of her. Her husband was making an effort to be present. She realized that she missed more than him being away from the family. She missed her partner, her lover. She moved her hand to the back of his head and ran her fingers through his thick black hair. She applied pressure with her hand and pulled his lips to hers.

Afterward, he expected to fall right to sleep, but that was not to be the case. Sleep came slowly and was not exactly restful. Dave kept going over whether he had created his own monster. Did he really need to work so much? Could he be more efficient and thus spend more time with the family that he loved with all his heart? He chased these thoughts throughout the night without any clear resolution, until he looked at the digital readout. It mocked his tired eyes announcing that it was 5:15. Resolved to get a head-start on the day, he got out of bed.

"Are you okay, honey?"

"Yeah, I just couldn't sleep. Go back to sleep, baby."

"No, I have the early shift and have to get up soon anyway. Coffee or shower?"

"You go ahead and take a shower. I'll get the coffee started."

Dave was starting to walk out of the bedroom when Debbie surprised him. She took his hand and pulled him in for a kiss. In the dim glow coming from the numbers of the alarm clock she looked him in the face and said: “I love you, Dave.” The kiss that followed was not a passionate one. It was a firm, steady kiss.

“Now that’s a nice way to start the day,” he said as they parted.

Chapter 5

Aiden felt the burn spreading through his chest and legs. It was a welcome feeling; it meant he was in the zone. Just four more laps and then a quick shower before school. Every morning he was in the pool doing laps. Training to make himself the best he could be. He didn't do it to beat the other swimmers. He did it to push himself harder and farther. It was something he couldn't tell others about. It would sound hollow to express his reasons in words. He simply had the drive burning inside him to become somehow better than he was. Oh, winning felt good and all, but it went much deeper than that. True, there were college scouts seriously looking at him and going to college was very important to him and his parents as well. The plan was to major in Business with a minor in International Studies and then putting that education to work in the corporate world. He already planned on it taking five years to complete and was looking forward to it. The scout for Berkley would be at the meet on Thursday, and he wanted to set a new personal best in both of the events he was in. Focus! As always, plan ahead, but take it one lap at a time. Do your best and learn from it, then do better! It was a mantra he had taken on board long ago.

As he touched the wall after the final lap, he looked up at his coach and friend Dominick. Dom had been his best friend since the 5th grade. He had transferred with his mom to Eagles Peak from

Seattle. They had hit it off from the start and still clicked. Granted, they had their differences over time, but their friendship always won out. They looked out for each other.

"Not bad," Dom said. "If you hadn't held back on the second to last lap, you would have been close to your PB. What were you thinking about?"

That was another thing that happened when you had been friends for so long. You knew each other too well sometimes. Dom was not one to pull any punches either. He called it like he saw it.

"You shouldn't worry about that scout. If you do, it will take your focus from what you should be doing, and you will not do your best. Let it go! You have trained your body and mind, and now all that is left to do is to go out there and DO IT! Now get your scrawny butt out of there so we won't be late for school."

Dominick was not what you would call swift in the water. It wasn't for lack of trying. He had taken lessons for years and had been on the swim team since the 6th grade. He knew his limitations and accepted them. Where he was a natural though, was on the boards. Dom was like an acrobat on the diving boards. He was naturally flexible and was fearless, as well as focused on the technical aspect of diving. In short, he was damn good and was likely to take State and be in the running for Nationals again this year. The two friends headed off for a shower and then the quick three-mile bike ride to school. It was a ritual they had done so many times they knew it down to the minute.

It was no surprise that they both sat down in homeroom just as the bell rang, not a minute early or late as usual. They had it down to precision timing as they also had with the rest of their daily schedules. They usually studied together after school, helping each other with the classes they were struggling with.

Aidan was a natural at math and science, and Dominick was good at history and literature. They didn't do each other's work, their integrity was too high for that to happen, but they did work together to understand the parts they were struggling with on their own. Because of this, they were both regulars on the honor roll. If all worked out as planned, then the dynamic duo would stay together at the University of California Berkley as well.

Julie was waiting for Aidan by his locker for lunch. While she was not part of the dynamic duo, she was definitely part of the inner circle. She had been friends with Aidan since kindergarten, and although they had drifted apart at times, they had always come back together. Theirs was not a romantic relationship, but it was a close one. Julie had often wondered why their relationship had never gone to the romantic level. She definitely thought Aidan was hot. Every girl at Smith High did. He was in great shape, had the kind of looks you saw in a magazine ad, and he was not like the other guys at school. The good-looking ones all seemed to know it and were stuck on themselves while Aidan did not appear to care one way or the other. He was simply a nice guy. He had gone out on dates with other girls, but as far as she knew, it never amounted to anything.

Maybe there was some truth to the rumor about Aidan and Dominick? She wondered for the hundredth time.

No, there couldn't be! She insisted to herself. If there were she would be the first one to know it.

Wouldn't she?

She spent a lot of time with both of them and, although they were very close friends, she never got that type of vibe off of them. Well then, if that was the case, then why had neither one of them ever made a pass at her either?

It wasn't like she was unattractive. At 5'6" and 110 lbs., with green eyes and honey blond hair, she knew that most boys, and even some men, gave her more than just a passing glance. She had always had plenty of guys asking her out, so it wasn't that.

Was it simply that they had been friends for too long?

Then again, maybe taking it to the next level wasn't the best thing to do. She didn't want to lose Aidan's friendship, and if things didn't go well romantically, then that was a risk she would be taking. No, she did not want to lose him. He meant way too much to her, and she hoped he knew it. That would have to be good enough, for now anyway.

"Hey, what's up?" Aidan asked with his typical nonchalance.

"What's up yourself? How did the test go?" she asked, referring to the big history test he had been studying for, and stressing over as well.

"To be honest, it felt good. Dom really knew what to focus on, and he worked with me quite a bit on the Civil War. I don't know why, but those dates would not stick in my brain. The word association he taught me to use actually felt like it worked. Anyway, I will know for sure tomorrow how I did. Until then I am just glad that test is over."

They settled into their old spot under the elm tree. The grass was soft and cool as they assumed their usual positions. He always sat with his back against the tree while she preferred to tuck her feet beneath herself and face him. As Aidan was pulling out his trusty ham on wheat, Julie surprised him by saying, "I have something for you. Since the test is over, I brought you a little something to celebrate. Before you say you can't, I know you have the metabolism of a cheetah." She unwrapped a small piece of a brownie. Aidan looked at his favorite treat in the whole world and silently appreciated her a little more.

"Julie, you know I can't afford to gain any drag before the meet." Meaning he couldn't afford to gain any weight.

"I know," she replied. "That's why it's a small piece, and you are going to carry my books home for me to burn off the calories." She batted her eyes at him. "It's the least you can do to pay me back for slaving away ALL night long in the kitchen for you."

"Thank you," he said as he looked directly at her.

She realized then that it was something he did not do all that often. She also realized that there was nothing that she liked more in the world than having Aidan Thompson looking at her eye to eye. She looked away and took a drink of her apple juice to try to get her heart back in its right place, instead of lodged in her throat beating about a million times a minute.

She sat up straight as a thought took hold of her.

"Aidan," she said, "why don't we go to the lake after the meet to celebrate your victory?"

"Whoa! Slow down there miss green eyes. Let's not get ahead of ourselves, shall we? You know I don't like to talk about the results of a meet before they are final. Besides, Tom Jenkins is going to be hard to beat in the 400. He's been chasing me every meet for the last three years, and now he has put on more muscle. I hear he's shaved his time down, some say by as much as two seconds. I don't know if it's true or not, but I'm sure there's some truth in it. I don't want to think that this is going to be a walk in the park and then have anyone take it away from me."

"Are you nervous about the scouts?" she asked.

"No, it's not that. They go off of the person and how well they have done over time, in more than a single event. Of course, they want to make sure that I don't choke under pressure, but I have had solid times all season long. I guess it's just that I am proud of my record and I don't want to give it away. I don't mind losing if I give it my best. I just don't want to lose because I got sloppy or lazy though. Do you know what I mean?" he asked as he absentmindedly pulled grass, one blade at a time.

"Well, when you put it like that, I sure do. You mean to say that you have an ego the size of a skyscraper and have trouble getting your head to fit through the doors of our pitifully small educational facility where you are forced to endure us day after day. We are so honored to be in your presence, Oh Great One!" She could not resist teasing him about his dedication. The smile on her face betrayed her though. She had been teasing him like this since he had begun winning races.

Aidan did not, even for a second, think of being offended by her words. He knew that she was his biggest fan, followed closely by Dominick and then his family. If there was one thing he didn't lack, it was support. He knew that there were a lot of people that supported him. He had become kind of a celebrity in Eagles Peak. He kept it all in perspective though because he was bright enough to realize that it was, in fact, a little world he was living in and sooner rather than later he would have to compete at a whole new level on the stage of life. Now there was a splash of cold water on his mood.

Julie could see the immediate change come over him. He went from smiling to reserved, in the blink of an eye.

"What's wrong?" she asked him.

"Just thinking about what's going to happen after high school," he said.

They'd had this talk before and would have it again. They were both thinking it through and freely discussed their fears and thoughts.

Julie did not want to lose him to this dilemma at this crucial point, so she brought him back to her question. "Well, superstar, you still didn't respond to my offer. Do you want to go to the lake after the meet?"

"I don't know. We both have that big Government test on Monday and should study for it."

As usual, he was right.

"Okay, I'll tell you what. Go to the lake with me, and I will come over, and we'll study together on Saturday. We will cram so much Government between our ears we will dream the Gettysburg Address."

At that, they broke out laughing just as the bell rang. Walking away from the tree, Aidan couldn't help but notice that Julie had definitely filled out nicely over the summer. He couldn't think of anyone ever looking better in a pair of jeans. There was no doubt about it. Julie was a fox of the highest caliber. For the millionth time, he repeated his mantra in his mind: focus, focus, focus!

Yeah, buddy! Easy to say when you aren't looking at something like that!

Well, then look somewhere else.

Right!

Saved by the door. Finally, they re-entered the school and soon were enveloped by the crowd going to their next class.

Aidan welcomed the distraction they gave him. More and more often he found himself thinking about Julie. He knew that he was falling for her, but he also knew that there was no point in it. She was more than likely going to Stanford, and he wasn't. He would probably be headed to Berkley. They were soon going to go down different paths, and he didn't want to distract her from her brilliant future. He knew he loved her. He had loved her for years and had admitted that fact to himself if to no one else two years ago. In the last couple of weeks though, he had started to wonder if he was falling *in* love with her.

There is a big difference between loving someone and being in love with them, he thought as he was buffeted on all sides by his fellow students who were going on their way to their respective classes as he rode the tide to his own class. He could handle knowing he loved her. That was easy to understand.

He couldn't think of anyone who didn't love Julie Ronowski. Okay, maybe Lisa Jackson. Since Julie beat her out for head cheerleader things had definitely soured between them. Other than that, though, she was more than liked by practically everyone. She was sincere, caring, and gorgeous to boot.

Oh yeah and the way she filled out those jeans!

That's enough of that already.

There are still two classes to go through today, and it would be very uncomfortable going around the rest of the day sporting a tent in your pants buddy.

With that thought, he looked around to see if anyone was paying any undue attention to his nether regions. It felt as if everyone must be able to see just how excited he was right then. As Dominick would have said, he was sporting some serious wood! Past experience should have taught him that people didn't notice things like that unless attention was brought to it. That knowledge did not make him feel any more comfortable. He wouldn't relax, as if, until he was safely in his seat, in the next class, with his erection hidden from view by his desk.

Chapter 6

Summer was sitting in U.S. Government class, half listening to Mr. Tanaka explain the reason for the separation of powers. The other half of her mind was busy thinking about Shawn Stephens. It took all her restraint to not turn her head and look at his handsome face. He had actually said hi to her.

"Summer, can you tell us why we have the legislative branch?"

"Um, well, it's to make sure that the laws passed by Congress and by the President as Executive Orders are not against the Constitution," Summer said.

"Good answer." Mr. Tanaka went on to explain how the Legislative branch functioned and she went back to daydreaming about Shawn picking her over her best friend, Sandy.

The bell for lunch finally rang, and Summer made her way to the cafeteria to meet her friends. As usual, the conversation was about how stupid the boys were which flowed into talk of who the girls thought was cute.

"Well, we all know who the cutest boy in town is," said Lisa. "Everyone knows Aidan is the cutest."

"Summer you are so lucky to have him as a brother."

Summer gave Lisa a strange look. "Are you serious?"

“You just can’t see it because he’s your brother. You have sister blinders on or something, but Aidan is *hot*!”

The other girls broke up into a fit of giggles. Part of it was from talking about someone being hot, but mostly because of the shocked look on Summer’s face.

“No, it’s because she only has eyes for Shawn Stephens,” said Karen. “Everybody knows you are crushing hard on him.”

“What do you mean everybody knows? Does he know? Who told him? I’m going to die?” Summer cried out. She buried her face in her hands and shook her head from side to side.

“No, stupid! Not literally everybody, just everybody with eyes in their head. One look at you when he’s around is enough to figure it out.”

Summer raised her head and slowly lowered her hands from her face. Her cheeks had a rosy blush to them. “If he finds out I’ll just die.”

“Oh, shut up already. That is exactly what you *do* want. If he finds out that you like him, then maybe, he will ask you to the dance.”

Summers' cheeks blushed even brighter, but she didn’t argue with Karen. In fact, the silly smile on her face showed how much she would like that to happen.

The conversation moved on to the other important topics revolving around their world of books, boys, and their budding fashion sense.

"Summer, can I ride with you to ballet?" asked Lisa.

"Of course, do you want to come over earlier and do our homework together?"

"Sure, that sounds good. I could use the help with math. Maybe you can help me make sense of Geometry."

Summer laughed. "Maybe we can figure it out together. I'm as confused as you are right now."

Chapter 7

Dave entered a quiet house and went to the kitchen to check the calendar on the refrigerator. Sure enough, Debbie had to work the late shift at the hospital. They all knew the routine well. The kids would be in their rooms working on their homework or, if that was done, doing something else quietly.

He never could understand how Debbie could do what she did. In the Navy, he had to pull his duty on late watches and had to modify his sleep schedule. Debbie did it all the time though. She must have just come from her shift and went straight to bed. He could never understand how she could just fall asleep when she wanted to. Dave's sleep cycle was set to a schedule, and if he deviated from it, he really felt the effects.

He checked his watch and saw that it was already after seven. He went up to Aidan's room and gently knocked on the door.

"Come in," Aidan said just loud enough to be heard through the door.

Dave went in and closed the door behind him, so their voices wouldn't travel.

"Did you guys eat dinner yet?" he whispered.

"I haven't yet. I just finished up with my calculus, and I still have a few pages to finish writing on my history report. I didn't realize it was this late already," Aidan said as he looked at his watch. "Are you going to make something, Dad?"

"Yeah, how does tortellini sound?"

"Great! Can you make a loaf of garlic bread too?"

"Of course. It'll be ready in about 20 minutes. I'll go see if Summer has already eaten. See you in 20?"

"Okay, thanks, Dad."

"Love ya, kiddo."

"Me too."

With that Dave left Aidan's room and went to tell Summer dinner would be ready in 20 minutes. He called out to her quietly through the door but got no response. Gently, he opened the door and waved his hand, before poking his head in. What he saw brought a smile to his face. His lovely little girl was dancing with her headphones on. She was totally oblivious to her Dad watching her.

When Summer noticed him standing there, she stopped her free dancing and took off her headphones. A lovely blush lit up her cheeks.

"How long have you been standing there, Dad?"

Dave put a finger up to his lips, "Shhhh."

"Only for a few seconds, honestly," he told her with the smile firmly tugging at the corners of his mouth. "I like to see you enjoying yourself. The reason I stopped in was to ask if you are hungry. I'm making some tortellini and garlic bread. Want some?"

"That sounds good," she replied. "Need some help?"

"Is your homework done?"

"Yes, Lisa stopped by after school, and we worked on it together."

Dave and the kids enjoyed a good evening together. They didn't really talk about anything serious. It was the fact that they were talking that was important. The laughs came easily, and before they knew it, it was time for the kids to go to bed.

Dave prepared the coffee machine and set the timer, so Debbie would have a hot cup of motivation ready for her. He left a sticky note for her on her coffee cup.

"Dinner/breakfast is in the fridge. I don't say it enough—I love you."

Chapter 8

A hospital is never a silent place. There's always a low hum of activity in the air. There are always nurses attending to their patients, dispensing medication on schedule, checking vitals. At night, the atmosphere is much more relaxed; if not silent, the hospital was subdued.

At this time of the shift, most of the nurses tended to gather around the desk. The patients were mostly asleep, and, except for routine tasks, things were very quiet. As usual, the gossip was flowing at a steady rate.

Debbie listened to the other nurses talking about the "Hot Doc" and whether he was married or single. This had become almost a routine conversation for the early morning gossip club.

"He doesn't wear a ring on his finger. Not even a liar's band on that long, strong finger of his," said Lisa with a faraway look in her eye.

Julie, ever the rational one chimed in, "Ladies, you know that a lot of the doctors don't wear their rings. It doesn't prove a thing. He could be married with a whole brood of kids at home."

"Well, I don't care if he is married. If he gives me a chance, I'm going to do him so good he would forget all about her," declared Rita, tossing her wavy black hair over her shoulder and pouting her lips.

That caused gasps and giggles all around. The girls were just being girls, and Debbie did not concern herself with the hallway gossip, even if it was fun to listen to, once in a while.

Of course, she knew who the "Hot Doc" was. There weren't too many doctors to choose from to begin with, and most of them were over fifty and at least forty pounds overweight. Yes, Doctor Jake Andersen was the type to turn heads whenever he entered a room. He was well over six feet tall, had blond hair, and eyes as blue as a glacier. Not that she had noticed, mind you. It was obvious that he worked out regularly. And to make matters worse, he was genuinely nice.

As fate would have it, Debbie had found herself working for Dr. Andersen quite a bit and quickly discovered that he was not only good looking and nice but also a very good doctor. He was one of the rare ones that were not only technically good but also had a nice bedside manner. His patients actually liked him, and so did the nurses who worked with him. This, of course, only fanned the flames of gossip. How could a catch like him still be single?

It was six months ago that he had started working at the hospital and, as luck would have it, more-often-than-not, their shifts matched up. Debbie had been pleasantly surprised at how easily they had settled into a routine, with a rhythm of its own, that both of them felt comfortable with. In time, Debbie and the good doctor began to talk about more than just work. This comfortable relationship was something they both enjoyed. They were patient-focused and dedicated to the job. It felt good to talk with someone, she reasoned, whenever she felt guilty about the budding relationship, and it wasn't like she was doing anything wrong. In fact, she had never even seen Jake outside of the hospital. If eating with a hundred other people around you in the cafeteria was a transgression, then that was the worst thing she was guilty of. In fact, Jake had never even so much as made a pass at her. He had kept the friendship to a working one, as had she, with distinct boundaries within the confines of the hospital. She always wore her wedding ring, so he knew she was married, but while they had talked about Summer and Aidan, they had never talked about Dave. Jake had never asked, and she had never brought him up.

The rest of the shift passed without incident, and before she knew it, the time for shift change was here. Debbie was briefing her relief on the status of her patients when she saw Dr. Andersen step up to the desk. Debbie stopped talking and turned to him to see if he needed her to do something.

"No, please, I don't mean to interrupt," he said, as he picked up the chart for the patient in room 338.

Debbie continued with her turn-over brief. When she was done, she looked around, but Dr. Andersen had left. Now, why did she feel a little let down by that? She made her way to the changing room to get her things and go home.

“Oh! Excuse me,” Dr. Andersen said, surprised as he stepped out of room 338. He barely avoided knocking her off her feet, by shifting to the side and grabbing her shoulders, and spinning her around. Debbie literally felt like she’d been swept off her feet. In truth, if it wasn’t for Jakes athletic reflexes that is what probably would have happened.

“I am so sorry. Are you okay?”

“Yeah, I’m fine. Nice moves by the way.”

“I guess the ballroom dance lessons paid off,” he said with a big smile.

“Really? Ballroom dance lessons?”

“My mom thought it was a good idea. In truth, it has come in handy over the years. You know weddings, Christmas parties, and hospital hallways. All of the standard occasions.”

“Well, thank you for the dance, kind sir,” Debbie said as she did a proper curtsy.

“You are quite welcome, my lady. Now, if you will excuse me, I must take my leave. Good day.”

“And a good day to you, sir.”

With that, Dr. Andersen continued with his rounds and Debbie went into the changing room. She felt light on her feet.

Chapter 9

Traffic was beginning to pick up on the commute to the office. Dave looked around while he waited at the stoplights and saw the same bored faces he had seen before.

When you take the same way to and from work each day, you tend to meet the same people doing the same routine as you. An easy nod of the head in acknowledgment to the people who were as much a slave to the grind as he was.

Judging from the looks on their faces they needed the rest as much as he did. It was a good thing it was the last day before a long weekend.

Yup, just another boring routine commute. Right, Mr. Bald man in the blue Accord? I'm sure you feel the same way, blond lady in the Toyota Camry with the five-hundred-yard stare. Are you going over the things you need to get done today? Maybe the dinner you are going to make for your family when you get home, he mused. *Maybe you are planning a date with an exciting lover. Or, more than likely, you are simply thinking about yet another long day ahead of you with too much to do and not enough time to get it done.*

Dave let out a long sigh. That was a thought he had grown all too accustomed to. It seemed to have become his life story. Too much to do and not enough time to get it all done. Maybe they would put it on his tombstone after he was gone.

> *"Dave was a good man.*
> *He worked really hard.*
> *There was always too much to do,*
> *and not enough time to get it all done."*

The light changed to green, and he moved along with his fellow commuters into another day in the world of business.

Turning off the road and into the nearly empty parking lot, he pulled into his reserved spot and retrieved his faithful traveling companion from the passenger seat. For quite a few years now his satchel was his only company on the daily trek to and from the office. It was a bit beat up but still worked well.

Dave reminded himself to stay focused on getting the audit done and wrap things up, so he could get home and help Debbie pack for the trip. The birds were starting to sing their early morning songs. The sound of his footsteps striking the asphalt sounded flat on the morning air as he crossed the parking lot and pushed open the side door to the building.

The morning went by without a hitch until 10:15 when Becky informed him of an emergency meeting of all department heads. Dave was fuming inside.

Crap. That is just what I do not need! Well, there's nothing I can do about it. He wrapped up the audit and sent out a couple of short important emails on what needed to be done.

The meeting was surprisingly short. It wrapped up in thirty-five minutes. On the way back to his office he remembered the promise he made to Debbie and thought about how he could delegate out some of this added workload without overburdening his staff.

Before he knew it, the day had somehow flown by, and it was now almost four o'clock. He went around to his people and made sure they were ahead of things before pushing them out the door, to start the long weekend. By the time that was done, it was already after five, and he still had a few more items to complete before he pushed himself out the door.

The next time he looked at the clock it was already going on nine o'clock. That can't be right! How can it be that late already? That was when he realized that Debbie hadn't called him. He quickly closed his office and said goodnight to the new man on security. On his way to the car, it started to rain and by the time he reached the shelter of his BMW he was part-way drenched and all the way out of breath. He put his satchel on the passenger seat and tried to catch his breath. He didn't like the way that he was breathing so hard after such a short and easy jog. He promised himself to start working out again. He wasn't getting any younger, and the signs were becoming obvious. The beginnings of a spare tire and breathing hard with only a light jog were only part of it. He was in his 40s now. *You are much too young to let yourself go like this!*

You need to take better care of yourself for the kid's sake, he scolded himself.

With his breathing more-or-less under control, he pulled out of the parking lot and merged into the flow of traffic, for the drive home. As usual, his brain shifted to autopilot, and he started going over the work he needed to do in his head. Just another typical night.

Chapter 10

Dave woke to the sound of banging. It seemed like it was coming from down the hallway. As the fog of sleep left his brain, he recognized other sounds. Debbie was breathing heavily. *She must be trying to wrestle the suitcases down the stairs*, he thought. Knowing he was in the doghouse for staying at work so late last night, he jumped out of bed and threw on his robe. He stubbed his toe as he hurried out of the bedroom and into the hall. The pain shot up his leg and he reached his hand down to hold his injured digit. He turned and rested his weight against the wall as he raised his eyes up to Debbie.

"Not very chivalrous, huh? Here I am rushing to your rescue and end up looking like a fool."

"Well, at least you are a chivalrous fool. A pretty handsome one at that. Move your hand and let me look at it."

Dave did as he was instructed.

"It doesn't look bad. Can you move it?" she asked.

He flexed it up and down, gritting his teeth from the pain.

"I don't think you broke it. Do you think you can walk on it?" she asked.

He tested it, gingerly at first, but then with more confidence.

"I think it'll be okay. It just hurt like a ..." He caught himself at the last second and looked at Debbie's face with her raised eyebrows.

"Once a sailor always a sailor, huh?" she teased him.

"I can manage the suitcases," he said.

"Okay but take it easy." She gladly stepped to the side and let him take over.

"That's the last of it. I've already packed everything else. Why don't you get dressed and I'll start making breakfast?" she told him after he had loaded the suitcases into the car.

They sat around the table talking about what they were going to do over the weekend. The kids were very excited to go see their grandparents.

"I can't wait," Aidan said cheerfully. "I bet I catch the biggest fish again this year."

"That is so gross," declared Summer.

"Fishing is not gross! It's so cool. You have to think about where the fish are, figure out what they want to eat, and then the fight at the end—wow!"

"No, the fishing part is cool. I like that part," said Summer. "It's the end where you have to ... *touch* them. They are so *gross* and *slimy*. Blech. Mom, will you go for a run with me on the trails?" she finished.

"Only if you promise to take it easy on me," Debbie replied, as she reached across the table and held her daughter's hand.

The moment held as Dave looked at his two beautiful ladies. "Come on, let's get on the road before it gets to be too much later," he said. "We're still a little ahead of schedule."

Debbie had told Dave before the kids came down, that she had finally given up waiting for him and went to bed. She said that she had heard him come in and take a shower. She just assumed that he was working late. She didn't call because she didn't want to interrupt him. "I know you wouldn't have stayed late unless you had to. I know you're working on cutting back on the late hours. I also know that sometimes it has to be done." She then gave him a kiss. "Now get the cereal bowls so we can get moving."

The rain had cleared out during the night, and it looked like it was going to be a spectacular spring day. Dave put on his sunglasses and started the car. The sun was already heating things up, and he felt a drop of sweat run down his chest.

"Summer, did you pack the sunscreen like I asked?" Debbie asked as she fanned herself with her hand.

"Yes, Mom. I even brought your spray bottle."

Debbie looked over at Dave. "Okay then, we're ready to go."

Dave backed out of the drive, and they were on their way. Things were looking up. All the lights turned green just for them, or so it seemed. Traffic was light, and they rolled out of town in good spirits. Dave could tell that even the kids were excited to be starting the trip. All of a sudden, Aidan called out, “Hey Dad, turn that song up!”

To Dave’s surprise, it was a song that he loved. He had grown up listening to it; it was one of his all-time favorites.

Debbie didn’t miss a beat as she started in:

“Hey Hey Baby
Don’t tell me I’m Crazy.
All I want to do is be with you, Daisy.
Daisy, Daisy, please be my Baby.”

Even Summer joined in. They were all singing along and having a great time. It was great being together. Dave was really looking forward to spending the weekend with his family. He knew that this was what it was all about. No matter how many projects he did right, or how many promotions he would get, it was this love of family that made it all worthwhile.

Of course, the singing and laughing didn’t last the whole trip. They eventually fell into their own little pockets of silence as people will do while traveling in a car, mere inches from each other. Aidan and Summer were in the back seat listening to their favorite music on their headphones, and Debbie was enjoying the scenery out of the passenger window.

The lushness of urban sprawl eventually gave way to fewer and fewer houses as they made their way into the hills. The trees were starting to show their new buds with the warmth that spring was bringing. They went through one stretch where the trees completely covered the road. It gave the impression of driving through a living tunnel. Dave leaned forward and looked out from the windshield, up into the natural canopy overhead. The diffused light was making a mosaic pattern on the hood of the car as they passed beneath it.

Aidan sat forward from the back seat and pointed. "Look at that squirrel." The squirrel was sitting on the branch like a prop from a movie set. The sun was shining on his fur, and he was busily munching on something. It was one of those remarkable moments that life gives you, if you take the time to witness them.

Summer took off her headphones long enough to ask what they were looking at. By that time, she had missed the squirrel, but Dave saw in the rearview mirror that she had turned her attention more towards the scene going by outside of her window.

A few miles later he looked in the mirror to check on his children. He tried to see what Aidan was focused on and smiled as he realized that he was about to fall asleep with his head on the door. Dave felt very content—he had his family with him and the whole weekend ahead of them. *This was going to be great; this was what life is meant to be. Not slaving away to the grind. Life was meant to be lived!* He thought to himself

He was splitting his attention between the road and the elegant curve of Debbie's neck. He felt a deep sense of peace.

Suddenly he jerked his attention back to the road. He had drifted dangerously close to the guardrail. Ok, so now he was not feeling so at peace. He decided his wife's neck would stay looking good by his focusing on driving. *Enough already! Focus on the road!*

He was grateful that Debbie didn't notice their near brush with the guardrail. She was busy looking at the swollen stream outside her window. The current was really moving, white mist rose in the air from the turbulent water. The ordinarily mild stream looked like a place to shoot the rapids. It was beautiful, but formidable. It had to be cold as hell.

After the shock had worn off, and his heart-rate returned to a somewhat normal level, he settled back into the comfortable routine of driving. They had made this trip at least twice a year for the last twelve years and were familiar with every twist and turn of the road. They favored taking this path less traveled instead of the interstate because of the scenery and the fact it only took about twenty minutes more to get to her folks' house. They both agreed it was a small price to pay for such a beautiful trip.

Dave felt himself getting sleepy and made plans to stop at the scenic overlook. Some places labeled 'scenic overlook' were anything but scenic; this one, however, was truly breathtaking. The lush pines made the scene look like life was always lush in this valley. The stream that cut through the thick carpet of pine, cut back and forth, as it made its way to where it would eventually join up with another river, on its path to the ocean. He remembered one time they had stopped there for a rest and a cloud bank had rolled in. It literally covered up the valley below them. They were still in bright sunlight but couldn't see anything of the valley floor far below. It was definitely worth stopping to rest for a little bit and take in the view.

Only five more miles and then a much-needed break, he told himself. He cracked the window, to let in some fresh air, and began to tap his fingers along with the song on the radio. The lack of sleep, over the past two days, was catching up to him. No problem, just a little bit longer and then a break for everyone. He sure could use the chance to stretch his old legs.

Chapter 11

They arrived at the lake house, in time to get settled in, before lunch. Before the car even stopped rolling, Sam, the golden lab, was announcing their arrival. Aidan stepped out of the car and was almost knocked to the ground by 70 pounds of pure happy, tail wagging, 'I am so excited to see you'—an emotion that only dogs can communicate. Well, dogs and small children, minus the tail wagging part. Summer ran from the other side of the car, wrapped her arms around Sam and was rewarded for her efforts with many wet doggie kisses. The kids rolled around with Sam for a few minutes while the adults said their hello's.

"I've missed you so much," Debbie's mother whispered in her daughter's ear, as they hugged each other tightly. Dave always loved the way they were so open with their love for each other.

His family had been much more reserved with their emotions, almost to the point of being cold. He knew his parents loved him in their way; it was just a distant way. He had quickly adjusted to the open embraces that Debbie's parents lavished on everyone they knew. He discovered that it was something that he had been craving his whole life and never knew it. Like so many things in his life, Debbie had shown him a better way of doing things. She had literally made his life better than he could have ever imagined.

Dave went straight to his father-in-law.

"How have you been, son?" her dad asked him, as they hugged each other firmly.

"I'm good, Dad." He paused and took a step back. He looked his father-in-law up and down. "You're looking good. Have you been working out?" Dave patted him affectionately on the shoulder.

"We've been watching what we eat and have started walking the trails together." He explained with a big smile on his face.

The ladies went into the house and the men got the things out of the car.

"Come on, kids," said Dave, "give us old men a hand, would you?"

"Old men? Speak for yourself! I'm still in the prime of my life," said the silver-haired, distinguished gentleman. In fact, even though the gray had taken over and the telling wrinkles around his weathered face told a story of their own, it was difficult to put an age to Jack Williams. He was a good-looking man at 5' 10". He was still solidly built, and his blue eyes still held a twinkle of mischief to them.

"So how are things?" asked Debbie's mother.

"Things are good, Mom." She was brought up short when her mother stepped in front of her and looked her in the eye. Debbie could never tell a lie when she looked into her mother's hazel eyes.

She finally broke eye contact, and they resumed their walk into the kitchen. She gave Debbie's hand a squeeze.

"It sure is good to see you again. It has been too long."

"For me too, Mom."

"The kids are getting big. Aidan's almost as tall as Dave now. I bet you have to beat the girls off him with a stick," she joked

"No, fortunately, he's more focused on swimming and soccer than the girls for now."

"Treasure this time sweetheart. I'm sure it won't last for long. Some pretty little thing will catch his eye, and he won't even remember how to spell his name, let alone be so focused on sports." She sat down at the kitchen table, still holding Debbie's hand. She gave it another affectionate squeeze. "I wouldn't be a bit surprised if he were already interested in a pretty little thing and just hasn't let you know about it yet." She gave her daughter a conspiratorial wink.

"Oh, you stop it now!" said Debbie "I already have enough to worry about."

"Well, he won't stay your baby forever you know."

They were interrupted by the sound of footsteps. Everyone knew where everything needed to go. That was one advantage of coming here, it was like a second home for all of them. Since Debbie was twelve, they'd been coming to this lake house. She had spent most of her formative summers here, and her children had spent theirs here as well. This was as much home as their own place. In some ways, even more so. It was where the family came together.

The boys decided to not waste any time and went through the ritual of checking the fishing gear and the boat out for an afternoon excursion. Once that was done, they dutifully asked the ladies if they would like to join them. Summer jumped at the chance, while the women decided to stay behind.

"I'll just ride along," she said. "I don't want to touch any of those disgusting worms or fish, but riding in the boat, sounds like fun."

To everyone's surprise, and Aidan's chagrin, Summer caught the most fish and the biggest bass that any of them could remember. It was an eight-pound large-mouth. "I didn't even have to touch any icky worms," she bragged. She had used a top lure that her grandfather had set her up with.

"Of course, it was not the lure that did the trick, it was her technique," Aidan insisted.

This only made her proud smile all the bigger.

Aidan, to his credit, didn't take any of the joy away from her. Inside, he was very happy for her. He was glad she came along with them, and he was happy to see her do so well. Of course, he had to act like he was disappointed, but everyone, except Summer, saw right through his act.

Fresh fish, a simple salad, some butter and herb potatoes, wine for the adults and soda for the kids rounded out an excellent dinner. After the table was cleared, they all went out to the fire pit, and they sat there as the sun went down into the waters of the lake.

The crackling fire kept them warm as they told stories and made jokes. In time, the kids made their way off to bed, their faces sticky with s'mores and, with stern direction from Debbie, to make sure they brushed their teeth before going to sleep. The adults had indulged as well, as attested to by the two empty wine bottles, and the opened third. The couples were cuddled together under blankets, not saying much, just enjoying the glow of the fire. It was not a silence that needed to be filled with words. In time, Jack patted his wife on the knee. "Come on beautiful, let's call it a night."

Dave and Debbie both stood up and wished them a goodnight. By mutual consent, they sat back down to enjoy the comfort of the fire, and each other, for a bit longer. It had been way too long since they had spent time together. *Really* together like this. Not watching a silly TV program or movie, not talking about the myriad things that needed to be done, and counting that, as spending time together, but enjoying each other's company, simply being a couple. This was good.

They watched the burning embers arc into the night sky, rising upon the heat of the fire below. The stars were clear on the black velvet backdrop. Stars like this couldn't be seen in the city, there were too many lights on. There was too much going on to actually see the galaxy the way it was meant to be seen. You had to slow down to really appreciate it. You had to *take* the time to look. Out here though, the stars were so clear you could almost reach out and touch them. To think that each and every one of those pinpoints of light could have planets circling them was more than a bit humbling.

Debbie's breathing settled into a regular, relaxed rhythm. He looked down at her lovely face. Her eyes were closed. He sat there with her head on his shoulder and just ran his hands gently through her long brown hair. *This is what life is really about*, he told himself. *This is the reason that I go to work so that I can enjoy these moments*. He had made up his mind. He was going to make some major changes in his life. He was going to quit working so many long hours and focus more on what he really loved.

Dave picked Debbie up and gently carried her into the house. He lay next to her for a long time in the bed, just looking at her. Sometime later, he too drifted off into a very peaceful sleep.

Chapter 12

Dave opened his eyes and saw that the early morning sun was brightening the room just enough for him to see. Debbie was still sleeping deeply, and he did not want to wake her up. He lay there for a little while, just looking at her beautiful face. She had her arm wrapped around his waist. He didn't want to disturb her, so he gently eased his way out from under her arm. He hesitated briefly before he unclasped his hand from hers. A loving smile was on his face as he turned away from his sleeping wife.

He found Jack in the kitchen.

"Feel like feeding the fish?" Jack asked him.

"Yeah, that sounds like fun. Let me go wake up Aidan."

"Okay, I'll make us some coffee," Jack said as he turned his attention back to the counter.

Dave decided to try to see if Summer wanted to get out of bed and come with them.

"No Dad, I'm too tired. I want to sleep a little more," she mumbled. She rolled away from him and buried her face in her pillow.

Dave kissed the back of her head. I love you, honey," he told her as he stood up.

"Love you too Daddy," she mumbled into her pillow.

When Dave returned, with a half-awake Aidan, they found bowls of cereal waiting for them along with a steaming cup of coffee for Dave.

"Aidan, I'm sorry, did you want a cup too? You are almost a grown man now."

"No, Grampa, I think I'll stick with the orange juice. I tried some coffee a couple of months ago. I believe that it is definitely an acquired taste."

The men just smiled knowingly at each other.

When Debbie woke up and finally made her way to the kitchen, she found Summer and her mom deep in conversation. The men had already left so the kitchen was all theirs. Debbie went to the coffee pot and poured herself a cup. She was surprised to hear her mom telling Summer a story about when she'd been a young girl. Summer was totally engaged in the story.

"So, who was it, Grandma? It was Grandpa, wasn't it? I know it was him. You two were in love at first sight! I just know it. There could have never been another for your heart, right Grandma?"

"Well, maybe not the only one for my heart sweet one. You see, the heart of a girl needs to grow. Usually, that happens in bits and pieces, from different loves and heartaches too. Very rarely do they all happen with the same boy."

"But for you they did, right? I mean you and Grandpa love each other so much." Summer looked to her mom for support.

Debbie arched her eyebrows and tilted her head towards her mom. This was her story to tell, and Debbie was not about to interrupt her. Plus, she was curious too. She had never talked about this with her mom.

"The first thing you have to realize is that the world was much different than it is today. My parents had grown up during World War II. They were young while it went on but their parents, your Great, Great, Grandparents, had lived with rationing and victory gardens. They had donated their belongings to the war effort. They were very frugal." She paused in her story for a bit, lost in her memories.

She shook her head and brought herself out of her past enough to continue her tale. "They were also frugal with their emotions." She paused briefly before continuing again. "Well, I was actually a couple of years older than you sweet one when it happened. You know that I grew up in Illinois, on a farm."

Summer nodded her head. She was leaning forward on the table, listening intently.

"Well, in the fall we had a fair to celebrate the harvest. It wasn't all that big, but it was nice. We had rides, games, and pig races." Seeing the surprised look on Summer's face, she quickly explained. "I know, it doesn't sound like it would be fun, does it? They had the little piglets all dressed up. Some of them were even wearing makeup. It was hilarious. There was also the atmosphere of the place. The men would bet on the winner, and there was real tension in the air. People were shouting and those little piggies, with lipstick and blush, all dressed up in dresses and overalls, were squealing and bumping into each other, fighting to get across the finish line so they could get to the food trough at the end. Well, I guess you had to be there to understand what it was really like. I guess the most important thing was that it was fun."

"I remember that it was really warm. I had tied my sweater around my neck, and it was making me sweat something terrible. I remember that there were four of us girls, but for the life of me, I can't remember all their names. I know Debbie Johnson and Lisa Watson were there. We were inseparable that summer." She got a distant look in her eye as she tried to bring back that day from long ago. "Julie? Or maybe it was Anne. No, that's not right either. Oh, that's right, it was Debbie's cousin from St. Louis. Now, what was her name? Oh, anyway her name isn't all that important. I'm sure I will remember it."

She brought the cup of coffee to her lips and took a drink, a long drink while she stared off at nothing. Summer looked at her mom and raised her eyebrow. Debbie just shrugged her shoulders. They both decided to let her take her time.

After what seemed a long time she resumed her tale.

"As I said, it was warm for that time of year and the four of us were together. I remember it was Debbie that suggested we go for a ride on the Ferris wheel. The smell of popcorn was in the air. We were walking down the center of the fair, towards the Ferris wheel when a little boy bumped into me knocking me off balance. I started to fall back when I was caught in his strong arms."

Both Summer and Debbie were eagerly listening to the story. She looked at the faces of her daughter and granddaughter and knew she had their attention.

"I was looking up at the handsome face of Bob Lewis. Bob was a senior and so handsome, and I had bumped into him. I was so embarrassed. He smiled at me. I guess he saw me blushing.

"Are you okay Gail?" he asked me.

"Wow! Bob Lewis knew my name," I remember thinking.

"Yeah, thank you for catching me."

He stood up and helped me to get my balance. He was wearing jeans, a white T-shirt, and a black leather jacket. His hair was thick and a darker black than his jacket. When he smiled at me, I swear my legs lost their strength.

"So, are you having a good time?"

"Um, yeah, we were just on our way to ride the Ferris wheel." As soon as I said it, I felt so embarrassed. He was a senior and here I was telling him that we were going on the baby ride, the Ferris wheel. I might as well have told him we were going on the merry-go-round. He was a senior, and I was a baby.

"That's cool. The Ferris wheel is my favorite ride," he said.

I looked at him, sure that he was joking with me.

"No, really. I like it up there," he said as he looked up at the top of the Ferris wheel. "You can see for miles."

Before I knew it, we were at the front of the line and my friends had run off saying that they all had to go to the ladies. I was so embarrassed.

Bob was really nice. As soon as my friends ran off on me, he told me that it was okay if I didn't want to go on the ride. I thought about it and decided that I would show them. I just knew that they were somewhere close and were watching to see what I would do.

"No, I want to go." I really liked the smile that broke out on his face. He was so handsome. He kind of looked like James Dean. Maybe it was the hair and leather jacket. I really don't know but to my young heart he was so cool, and he wanted to be with me."

We talked about school. We talked about the football team. We talked about things that didn't matter much. I guess he could tell I was nervous. It was the first time I had been alone with a boy, to be honest. I was so nervous until I looked out and saw the view from the top. I could see the lights of the town to the left of us. Now I understood what Bob had meant when he said he loved it up here.

All of a sudden, our car jerked to a stop.

"It's okay," he reassured me. They are probably just letting some people off. We'll be moving again in no time, you'll see."

I was startled when he put his hand over mine and leaned towards me. "If you look over there," he said pointing to the northern part of the town lights, "you can see the school."

Once he pointed it out things began to fall into place. In no time at all, I saw where my home was. It was like I was seeing my town for the first time. I never knew it could be this beautiful. From up here, it looked like a big beautiful painting.

"It's beautiful," he said.

I turned to look at him. I was shocked. It was like he had read my mind.

"It's not as beautiful as you are though."

Suddenly, he was kissing me. At first, I was too surprised to appreciate what was happening. This was my first kiss. I remember that the surprise passed quickly, and I realized that I liked it. He was still holding my right hand and gently kissing me. I remember his lips tasted like buttered popcorn.

The wheel turned again. We kissed some more. The ride ended. I was afraid that he had only gone with me to see if he could get the young girl to kiss him.

Gail stopped her story and took a long drink of her coffee. She was staring off at nothing, lost in her thoughts.

Debbie looked at Summer. Both of them wanted to hear more but didn't want to interrupt her. As the seconds turned to minutes Summer couldn't contain herself any longer.

"So, what happened then, Grandma? Come on! You can't stop the story there. What happened next?"

Gail brought herself back from her memories and looked at her daughter and granddaughter and smiled. "Oh, it isn't all that interesting a story." She said, lowering her gaze to her wrinkled hands.

Debbie smiled and looked at Summer. “I don’t know about you, but I’m very interested.

“Me too! I want to hear what happened next. Come on Grandma, tell us please.”

“Well dear, since you said please, I will. Promise me though, if my story becomes too boring you’ll let me know, okay?”

Summer dutifully nodded her head.

“Well, Bob was interested in more than a stolen kiss at the top of the Ferris wheel. We stayed together into the night. I remember he won me a teddy bear on some shooting game.” She paused again, lost in the memories. “You know, I think I still have it up in a box in the attic.”

“I remember it was getting colder as night fell. Bob put his jacket on me.”

“Bob, I can’t wear your jacket. People will think I’m your girl.” I said to him.

“Well, will you?”

I was sure he was teasing me now. This had to be some kind of joke. I was a sophomore, and he was a senior. It had to be a joke. I turned away from him, so he wouldn’t see how upset I was.

“Gail,” I felt his hand on my shoulder, “I mean it. Will you be my girl?”

I couldn’t believe it. He was really asking me to be his girl. It wasn’t a joke. I just nodded my head, and he put his jacket around my shoulders. It was so big on me, but it felt so good.

Gail paused in the telling of her tale again. She didn't move. She didn't pick up her now cool cup of coffee and take a drink. She just sat there. Her gaze was focused on that long-ago time. After all this time she could still remember how she could smell him on that jacket.

Summer couldn't take it any longer. "So, what happened to him, Grandma?"

Gail sat there for a minute longer without turning her head. She didn't move at all. Her gaze was still focused far away when she answered her granddaughter in a quiet voice. "He died, honey."

Gail looked at Debbie. "Honey, would you freshen up my cup? It seems to have gone cold."

"Of course, mom," said Debbie. She put her hand on her mom's shoulder as she walked by her.

Debbie poured fresh coffee and put cookies on the table before sitting back down.

After a little bit, Gail went on with her story. She reached across the table and took Summers hand. "This is the part I think you have been waiting for dear one. Your Grandfather and I were both going in our junior year when Bob died. Grandpa lived a couple of houses down from mine. We had always been friends but had kind of drifted away over the last year." She paused briefly and tilted her head. "No, that isn't quite right. I drifted away from him. I spent more time with my girlfriends, but I remember him always being there. My friends didn't know how to deal with me. I remember that they kind of faded away that summer, but Jack was there for me." She looked at her daughter and her granddaughter. "That sweet man has been there for me for all my life."

They sat around that table for a few minutes, drinking coffee and eating cookies, lost in their own thoughts.

Summer looked at Debbie, "please tell me about your first kiss, Mom." When Debbie hesitated, Summer began to plead with her. "Come on Mom, I am sure that it was totally fantastic." Debbie looked at her mother and raised an inquisitive eyebrow. They both had seen the quick blush rise in Summer's cheeks. Finally, Debbie gave in and told her about her first love. While it was not a love of epic proportions, it was sweet, and more than a little revealing of the girl Debbie had once been.

"When I was a girl, I was a little reserved."

"Oh, be honest with her Debbie. You were a shy girl who was more comfortable with her books than with people."

"Okay, Mom, I see that I am not going to be able to embellish even a little bit. Well, I will try to tell my tale without embarrassing myself too much."

"Oh, I seriously doubt that is possible. This very topic is sure to embarrass, but please continue, my sweet child."

That was exactly what Debbie felt like all over again. She felt like that little girl. She felt the doubt, fear, hesitation, and joy that she had experienced on that day so long ago. "Let me just start with telling you that it was not your father. Most of my friends had already kissed a boy, and they had told me all about it. I felt that I was ready. I had even practiced in front of a mirror." Debbie puckered up and acted like she was in a passionate, yet chaste kiss, and after the giggles had died down, she continued. "He was a boy that I had known for years. We had grown up together and had been best friends for a long time."

"I knew it! It was Tommy Smithton. I always thought there was more there than friendship."

"Mom, please, this is my story."

"Sorry, honey, I always had my suspicions, but I didn't want to push."

Debbie couldn't help herself, and she laughed. It was a weird feeling, talking about this thing that she had kept a secret from her mother for so long. Lines were definitely being crossed. It was a good thing.

"Well, as you know, Summer, behind Grandma's house there is a creek that runs back into the woods. Tommy and I, like I said, were best friends. We were the same age, and we liked the same things."

Debbie's mother interrupted her. "No dear, I don't think that is exactly correct." She took a sip of her coffee. "I think that, in most things, Tommy did what you wanted to do to make you happy. You were just too innocent to see it for what it was."

Debbie thought for a minute. She cast her memories back in time and, now that her mom had said that, things clicked into place in a different pattern than she had remembered them. She compared the two possibilities and, in the end, came to the conclusion that it did not matter. They had enjoyed each other's company regardless of who had followed whom. At the end of the day, they had done the same things. In-spite-of that enlightened conclusion, she did look at things differently now. She decided to not let this new insight change the innocence of her tale.

"It was a warm summer day, and we went down to the creek, to see if we could catch some crawfish."

"Ew! That's disgusting!" Summer said. "I can't believe that you would touch those nasty, slimy, squirmy things."

"Child, sometimes I wonder if you are my daughter after all. Mom is this the result of some distant part of our family tree?" Debbie asked looking at Gail. "I know for a fact that you are not afraid to get your hands dirty. I have seen you bait a hook with a squirming worm without batting a pretty eyelash. In fact, there are no women in our family that are so against getting their hands dirty."

"Mom, that isn't fair, and you know it," objected Summer. "I don't have a problem getting my hands dirty. Dirt doesn't bother me. It is those slimy, nasty things that gross me out."

"Oh, well then, the matriarchal line is saved from extinction. We will persevere in the end. In the lives of women, there is only dirt to be soiled upon our dainty hands. There are no, what did you call them, nasty, slimy, squirmy things? Child, just you wait until you have a child of your own. It pretty much immunizes you from that fear," Gail informed her. She then rolled her hand as a signal for Debbie to continue with her story. She really wanted to hear Summer's story, having already pretty much figured out how her daughter's tale would go from here.

"Okay Mom, like I said, it was a warm day, and we were catching crawfish. Other kids joined us and then went on their way. After a while, we decided to take a break and went upstream a ways. There was an area where the trees were thicker. Tommy had brought along some sandwiches and a couple of pops to drink. After we finished the sandwiches, we laid on the ground and looked at the light as it filtered its way through the leaves. I remember the sun was warm on my face and I was happy to be there. I felt Tommy's hand move next to mine. I didn't think much of it. We had bumped hands too many times to count. In fact, we had bumped into each other in many confusing and embarrassing ways. That was what happened when you were best friends, right? Anyway, he made his move and went from brushing hands to holding my hand. I was surprised but decided not to pull away. It felt nice."

Summer looked at her mom and saw the distant look of someone that was lost in a time that was past and not yet so far away. She saw a small smile on her face as she was lost in her story. Summer was surprised by how much love she heard in her mother's voice as she told the tale of the boy she had first fallen in love with.

"I was happy, holding his hand and watching the light filter through the canopy of leaves overhead. The smell of the woods mixed with the earthy smell of the ground and the feeling of Tommy's warm, callused hand was a very good thing. Tommy propped himself up on his elbow and looked down at me. I remember like it was yesterday, how I became sure he was going to kiss me. I just went with it."

Debbie just looked at Summer.

"Oh no, you don't Mom! You don't get off that easy, and you know it. How was it? Was it earth shattering? Earth-shaking? Or just awkward? Don't hold back! Dish, Mom!"

"If you insist, sweetie," Debbie said with a sweet smile on her lovely face. "But remember that what comes around goes around."

An instant blush rose on Summers' cheeks.

"It was sweet and innocent, at first," Debbie said with a gleam in her eye. "As we settled into it, the kiss became more passionate. But that was when I broke it. I didn't want it to go any further than that. I don't think he really did either. He put me too high on a pedestal. He really thought that I could do no wrong. It was only puppy love, but it was oh so sweet while it lasted."

Debbie looked at her mom, and then they both turned to Summer and said together: "Your turn!"

With a severely red blushing face, Summer told her story about the first time she had let Shawn kiss her. The memory was still fresh because it had just happened a few weeks ago.

After another half an hour or so of girl talk Summer talked Debbie into going for a run with her, Debbie agreed on the condition that Summer take it easy on her. To Debbie's credit, she made it for a complete lap around the lake before she stopped to catch her breath. Gail had been waiting for them by the dock and joined Debbie. They walked at a comfortable pace around the lake, enjoying their easy conversation.

"There she goes again," said Jack. "Doesn't that child ever get tired? That's the fourth time I've seen her go around. It takes me about thirty minutes to walk that loop. That means it must be more than a mile each lap."

"I tried to keep up with her a couple of times," confessed Dave "I held my own for a little while. I swear though, once I dropped off, she kicked it into another gear. I really think she was holding back, taking it easy on me."

"Lucky you," said Aidan. "I ran with her when she first joined the track team. She wanted to run the mile like me. I knew she was good, so I told her sure. I made the mistake of taking it easy on her. It was her first time, and I didn't want to embarrass her. I thought she was starting out too fast, so I told her to back it off or she would run out of steam. She told me that she was okay, she said she knew what she was doing. I figured she would start to fade at the half-mile point. Like you said Dad, she kicked it up into another gear. Before I knew it, I was running at my race pace, and she didn't look to be tiring at all. I knew people were watching us by now. We were starting the last lap, and she kicked it up another notch. Dad, I had to really stretch out my stride and dig in. In the end, I finished maybe a stride ahead of her. I can't even say for sure if she didn't hesitate at the end, just so I would cross the line first. Well, that was almost a year ago now, and I can tell you without any embarrassment that she can outrun me, and everyone else on the team."

Right then Summer came out of the trees on the back side of the loop and waved at the boys. She slowed down just short of the women and joined them for their walk.

"I lost count dear, how far do you think you ran?" asked Gail.

"I think it was a little over five miles Grandma."

"Do you usually run that far?"

"Five miles is a good distance. It's long enough for me to get warmed up and then push myself."

Back out on the water, the boys had decided that they had caught enough fish for a good dinner. In reality, Dave had looked at his watch and saw that it was time to come in. They would have just enough time to get the fish cleaned and have dinner on the table by six. Through long experience, he knew that his in-laws liked to eat on a schedule and he didn't want to put them out in any way. This had been a great weekend so far.

Dave was brought out of his own thoughts by his father-in-law's voice. "How is the job going, son?"

"It's going well, Dad. In fact, there is some talk about expanding the department."

"Would that mean that you have to work longer hours?"

They had talked about how much Dave worked over the years. Jack had never pushed him. He was there as a sounding board, and they both knew it. He had sacrificed his time at the grindstone until he retired. Now that he had pulled back, he realized how much he had missed.

"Funny you should mention it. I didn't want to say anything, but I am working on a plan to spread the workload out a bit. I should be giving more responsibility to some of my more senior people. It will help to groom them to step up to leadership roles and take some of the load off me."

Aidan watched the exchange between his father and grandfather. He really hoped it would work out that way. He liked spending time with his dad. They really got along well. Aidan knew through experience that these good plans did not always pan out. He had come to expect it. After all, it was a man's job to make sacrifices for his family. In the end, it was himself that was sacrificed.

Dinner turned out great. The boys had a good time in the kitchen while the ladies relaxed on the porch. Fried fish, corn on the cob, and watermelon for dinner. Of course, more smores by the fire.

The kids caught fireflies and put them in a couple of jars with holes in the caps.

After a good night's sleep and a big breakfast, they got back on the road for home. It had been a great weekend.

Chapter 13

Dave woke up disoriented. He looked around and realized he had been sleeping in the guestroom. He couldn't remember why he would have been sleeping there instead of in his own bed. He didn't remember having a fight with Debbie, he didn't remember going out with his friends and coming back after having a couple too many. Then again, he thought, he did have a splitting headache. The light coming in through the blinds made it feel like daggers were stabbing into his head. He felt dizzy. Spots danced across his vision. He closed his eyes and took some deep breaths hoping the agony would pass. He pressed his hands down on the sheet in an attempt to feel grounded.

His head was all foggy. He couldn't seem to concentrate on anything. His thoughts were flitting from one thing to the next with no logical connections. Nothing was making any sense. His throat closed down and a metallic taste flooded his mouth. He fought down a strong urge to vomit. The room was spinning. He pressed his palms down harder and concentrated on taking small breaths.

After a while, he felt he had himself under control. He sat up and immediately regretted it. A new wave of nausea hit him. He clenched his eyes tightly, taking small quick breaths.

Well, maybe I did drink too much last night after all. He braced his arms out to the side to prevent himself from tipping over. Once the bright flashes had quieted down behind his closed eyelids and his head had stopped spinning, he dared to crack his eyes open again.

Okay, that's a little better, he told himself. In time, he was able to stand up, and make his way out of the guestroom.

He looked around the living room and didn't see any telltale signs of a night of excess; there weren't any empty cans sitting on the coffee table. He followed the smell of coffee into the kitchen.

Everything seemed to be in order here as well. He was sure the mystery would be solved when Debbie told him all about the errors of his ways.

The metallic taste in his mouth was still strong. His tongue felt very thick, and his throat was really dry and raw. It felt like he'd vomited. Now that he thought about it, his muscles felt really weak too. Maybe he was coming down with something.

He poured a cup of coffee and brought it to his lips to take a drink. He coughed and sprayed some of the coffee out of his mouth and all over the kitchen table. He put the cup on the counter, spilling half of the hot liquid onto his hand. He grabbed onto the edge of the counter for support. He gripped it tightly and waited for the coughing fit to pass. He stayed that way, his arms braced and his hands gripping the edge of the counter, gasping for air. He was afraid to let go. He had a strange feeling that if he didn't hold tight, he would drift away. In time, he got himself back under control. He kept taking short breaths until his stomach settled down and he was reasonably confident that it would not exhume last night's meal all over the floor.

He definitely did not feel well. He sat/fell down onto a chair at the kitchen table.

It looks like I am going to have to call in sick, he finally admitted to himself. That was something he hadn't needed to do in years. *I'll just rest my eyes here for a minute.* He lay his head down on his arms and quickly dozed off.

He didn't have a restful nap. His dreams were a mass of distorted sensations. He heard faint voices but couldn't make out what they were saying. He kept hearing a rhythmic beeping. It sounded like the garbage truck backing up. No, that wasn't exactly right. Well, it was something close to that.

He felt the pressure in his head increase. He dreamed that his head had turned into a big red balloon that kept inflating. It kept getting bigger and bigger until his dream shifted. He was now lying on a beach, at the surf-line. The waves came in and crashed over his body. He thought it strange that he was wearing a hospital gown and lying on a beach. Curiously he didn't feel embarrassed to be so revealed. He felt entirely at peace. The waves weren't big, and when they crashed over his legs, it felt terrific. The feeling of the wet sand slipping through his fingers was nice as well. He relaxed more and drifted deeper into his dreams. He felt the sun on his body, and he felt drawn to the warmth.

Chapter 14

Things at work were going well. The changes Dave implemented in his department were taking effect, his team had stepped up to the additional challenges and were performing better than he had hoped. The morale in the department had never been higher.

Things were going so well that Jim, Dave's boss, had put him in for a bonus. He even found himself leaving the office at a decent hour and, as a result, found himself more engaged at home.

He was going to the kids' activities and had found that he really enjoyed watching them in their environment. Before, he had pretty much only seen them at home and when they went places together as a family. He had never really been with them as they interacted with their peers; he didn't know that they had such competitive sides to their personalities. He quickly found out that both Aidan and Summer were gifted athletes.

Aidan had a sense for the players around him on the soccer field. It wasn't just his vision of the field, it was his anticipation of what they were going to do, that allowed him to be in the right place more-often-than-not. He fed off his team-mates, and they fed from him as well. At times, Dave thought they looked like raptors from the movie *Jurassic Park*. They circled their prey until it was time to pounce, and then they did so as a unit, with great precision. It was really something to see.

That friend of his, Dominic, really had a burst of speed that was deceptive. He would be running along and then all-of-a-sudden, he was off like a bolt. They had a pre-set play where, Aidan would feed it to where he knew Dominic would be, and the defending team could only try to react quickly enough. They usually failed. If they were successful, then Dominic would lob the kick up higher instead of blasting it into the goal. Aidan would be streaking in from the wing and either take the shot on goal or clear it out again depending on how the defense had set up to the play. Either way, they were wearing them down, and the defense was showing their hand. The analogy of raptors was very fitting, Dave decided.

Aidan was also very dedicated to his swimming. Every morning he was up early for his training and Dave went with him a couple of times to the pool. Dave was a good swimmer, but Aidan was much better. His well-muscled frame cut through the water with ease.

Summer was dancing and running. She was training with the ballet school, and she was also on the cross-country team. She felt that the two sports were complementary, and Dave could find no reason to fault her reasoning. Both sports required strength, endurance, and a strict adherence to discipline. All of these things, Dave had learned, his little girl had in abundance. The little girl that he had held on his lap and read stories to had grown into a fierce competitor.

She was always practicing one of the two disciplines. She could be found stretching while doing her homework, literally she would be doing the splits with her literature book open in front of her concentrating on Shakespeare. Running was her true love though. It was the area that she really excelled in. Her family could always tell what her day of the week was—her coach made her take a rest day once a week and that was the day that she was grumpy. She really hated not being able to go for a run, but she understood that her body did need a break. She compensated by making the day before, her hardest training day of the week. It was usually her long run, but sometimes she mixed it up and made a grueling integral day, as she called it.

Dave was doing better on his promise to get in shape himself. He was up to running a 5K without stopping. He wasn't setting any speed records, but he had come a long way from getting winded by running to the car. He was also doing push-ups and sit-ups in the morning. The exercise, coupled with watching what he ate, was having an effect he could finally see in the mirror. He was definitely trimming down. He was down another notch on his belt. Dave had talked about his new exercise plan with his doctor on his last visit, and he had given him some good advice.

"Remember Dave, you didn't get out of shape overnight. You worked on that for years. Getting back in shape is going to take time too. Don't expect overnight success. You are doing the right things. Keep doing them, and you will notice the improvements. You will also feel better as you enjoy a healthy life."

Everything was looking up, except for his relationship with Debbie. They had both made an effort, but it felt like there was something that was keeping them apart.

Dave had cut back his hours at the office. Most of the time he was out of the door by five, there were some days when that was just not possible, days that he just could not get out the door on time. *That was to be expected though, right?* He was the head of the department, he reasoned. There were some times that he had to earn his salary and just had to suck it up. It couldn't always be how he wanted it. Sometimes things had to be done, and sometimes that meant working long hours. The difference was that now he was keeping a record of the overtime in his head and he was making a conscious effort to keep the balance. When he put in the long hours, he would make up for it by leaving early when things had calmed down. He made a point to let his team know when he was leaving early, he did not want his team to think that he expected them to work the long hours just to meet the standard. The standard was to get the job done during the normal working hours.

No, the overtime at work was not the issue this time. This time, it was something else that was going on. Maybe it was just that they had been together so long. *Maybe this and maybe that! Maybe anything and Maybe nothing at all. Stop it already and get your mind back on the task at hand. Focus and get this done*, he told himself.

Dave leaned forward and focused more intently on the spreadsheet before him. He was happy things were going better, but he felt increasingly frustrated about Debbie. His mind would keep wandering back to the distance that was growing between them. It was like after you had bit your tongue. Before it was hurt, you never paid much attention to that part of your body. Once it was hurt though, you focused on it more and more. That was what had happened to Dave. When the relationship had been stable, he hadn't given it much thought. To be honest, he'd taken it for granted. He went to work, did a good job, and expected to find the love of his life home when he was able to slay the dragon and return to their castle.

Lately, he felt that even when the love of his life was home, she wasn't really there. It was like she was going through the motions, she was doing what was expected of her. She wasn't happy, and Dave knew it.

Focus, Dave! he scolded himself. If he wanted to leave on time, he had a lot to do in a little bit of time, but his eyes invariably strayed to the pictures on the corner of his desk. The new one of all of them sat next to the one that had been there for years. His father-in-law insisted on using the tripod and timer, so they could all be in the picture this time. His exact words had been, "Family should be together. We should not leave someone out just to hold the camera. Family stays together."

What great words: "Family stays together." Some said that it was an old-fashioned sentiment. *Well, then I am just a bit old-fashioned.* With a smile on his tired face, Dave once again bent to the task of slaying this particular dragon.

Chapter 15

This is not going to be a good day, Aidan said to himself as he swung his legs out of bed. He felt heavy. This sense of weight, he knew would likely not go away. In the past, no matter what he had tried to do on days when he woke up feeling like this, everything felt heavy no matter how hard he tried to shake the feeling. It was harder to get into his run or laps, it was harder just to walk from class to class. The only thing re-assuring about feeling this way, on a day as important as this, was that he had broke his own record in the 400 on one of these "heavy" days.

Since the meet was scheduled to start in a few hours, he kept his morning run easy and let his mind go over his plan of attack for the day. The butterfly, second in the relay, then the 400. Then off to the lake with Julie and Dominick and the rest of his friends. He was looking forward to seeing Julie in her simple black one-piece that she somehow transformed into the sexiest swimsuit ever, the way that it rose up her hips and wrapped around her perfect butt.

ENOUGH ALREADY!

Picking up the pace to match his already labored breathing he clearly had some issues to work out, and the best way to take care of them, in the short term, was with a cold shower.

FOCUS ALREADY!

This is a big day, and as sexy as her ass is it will not help you to focus on what you need to be thinking about. There will be plenty of time to feast your eyes on her figure after the meet! Now get with it already.

Dominick was already at the pool and doing his warm-ups. "What's up, bro?" Dom called out.

"I feel heavy today," Aidan replied

"Well then, we need to get the lead out, so move your ass and get in the water!" Dom barked at him with a big smile, showing just how serious he was.

Aidan jumped in and wasted no time in settling into a comfortable breaststroke to loosen his muscles. *Don't push it*, he told himself. *Focus on the form and let the time take care of itself.* This was the mantra he always told himself while preparing for a race. It was one of the first lessons he'd learned when he joined the swim team. So far, it had worked for him, and he saw no reason to change what worked now.

As he pulled himself up on the side of the pool, Dominick said to him, "For someone feeling heavy you sure don't swim like it. I know you're taking it easy, and you are still faster than me."

"I'll take that as a compliment bro," he replied. "I don't know why, but I just feel like something is holding me back today. I can't put my finger on it, but I haven't completely shaken it yet either."

"Have no fear, Dominick is here! I will lift your spirits through my comic wit. By the time we get to school, you'll feel lighter than air my friend."

At that, both friends burst out laughing.

"You are so full of shit Dom," Aidan said.

"Yes, I am," Dominick said proudly. "All great comedians are full of shit. It's what fertilizes our lush imaginations."

At that last bit of Dom-ism they both lost it and laughed till tears were coming from their eyes. Aidan shook his head in wonder at the way Dominick had of making him laugh. Go figure! He was right after all. He didn't feel heavy anymore. They actually had to stop twice on the ride to the school because they were laughing so hard. If they had kept on riding one, or both of them, would surely crash into something or simply fall off their bike.

Once they got to school, they went to the showers to run some hot water over their muscles to keep them warmed up.

With the smell of chlorine in the air, the background voices of the crowd fades as the focus becomes more on what needs to be done instead of on what was going on around him. The sound of his heartbeat and his relaxed breathing are the only sounds that matter until the piercing sound of the whistle cuts through his concentration and he launches himself into action. His body slices into the cold water. *Controlled kicking 13, 14, 15, clear the surface and stroke 1, 2, 3, 4, breathe, focus on form and forget about the time. This is my race. I will swim it my way. Breathe. Legs straight and toes pointed.*

Pull forward with the arms. Coast after the stroke then propel forward. Technique is what wins races.

Aidan opens his eyes and lets them drift to where they always do. Right there, in the middle of the stands, Julie sits with his parents. They share a look then he slowly nods his head. That's his signal to her that he's ready. He's rewarded with the smile that makes him have to remember to breathe again. He doesn't show it though. He lowers his head and waits for the call to the platforms.

He continues to go over the race in his mind, thinking through all the details from the launch, to the turns, to the final reach. Every detail, every motion, and every possibility he tries to think of in advance. That way, when it's time to do it, he won't have to think about it.

The first two races he's already won. They are over and don't matter for now. He's pumped up and ready to go for it once again. This is his favorite event, and his record shows it.

Finally, the call to the platforms is sounded, as he approaches, he sees David Jenkins who will be swimming in lane four. Jenkins has been chasing him for the last two years, and he has come very close to winning more than once. Somehow, Aidan has always come out on top. Jenkins looked like he had been spending a lot of time in the gym. His shoulders and chest were much more defined, and he looked like he had grown four or five inches since the last race.

Ok, Aidan, don't get yourself psyched out because he looks like he can bench a small car. Remember this is your race and you will swim it how you want. Technique is the key to speed. Focus, Focus, Focus!

His vision closed-down to the spot he would hit the water. His focus was on the point where he will surface, his fingers were reaching for the wall. The starting whistle cuts shrilly through the air.

A quick look at the clock confirmed how he'd felt he did. It was a new personal best. He looked up to the center of the stands. The look on Julie's face was hard to read. She looked like she couldn't believe it. A quick look at the scoreboard revealed the cause of her disbelief.

I ... lost? By a 10th of a second?

A quick flashback of the race told him the story. Technically, it was a good race. In fact, he'd beaten both his personal best and set a new school record. Jenkins had simply swum faster; he earned the win. With that Aidan began to smile as he climbed out of the pool and walked over to where Jenkins was being congratulated by his teammates. When they saw Aidan approaching, they fell back, not knowing what to expect. The photographer from the Daily Telegraph caught the scene in perfect detail. Aidan stepped up to Jenkins and shook his hand, congratulating him on his win and new record. Aidan was very surprised by all the attention his handshake caused. It was on the front page of the paper the next day and even earned a small comment on the 10 o'clock news that night. But his dad had to tell him about it the next day because he'd been too busy to notice.

Chapter 16

The day could not have been more beautiful, the sky was clear, and the wind was light, out of the south at three miles per hour, keeping the heat of the sun at bay.

Aidan, Dominick, and three other boys from the swim team arrived at the turnoff for Lake Barker shortly after four o'clock.

"Take it slow," Dominick said, "this old girl can't handle the ruts like she used to."

"I know, I know," Aidan shot back. "I won't hurt your old girl."

"Actually, she's not old," replied Dom, "she's a classic."

"Yeah, right! So, you keep telling us!" Aidan joked.

"Look," Jason said from the back seat. "It looks like the party has started without us."

A little further up the road, the trees receded, revealing a picnic area that was familiar to all the kids. There were seven cars already there and the music announced to all around that the party was well underway. Most of the people were gathered around Tank's truck. No surprise there, everyone knew where the beer was.

Tank had rigged his truck to hide a keg inside the toolbox on the back of the bed. Of course, the local police also knew about it, it was one of the oldest tricks in the book, but they turned a blind eye as long as the party was kept to a dull roar and people drove home safely.

As Aidan parked the car, Tom Peterson started clapping, and soon the whole crowd joined in like they were welcoming a conquering hero.

Slightly embarrassed, Aidan went forth into the crowd with a silly smile plastered on his face. That is, until he saw Julie tanning herself on the dock, and at the sight of her, his smile turned into a full-fledged high watt affair.

He returned the energetic high-fives as he made his way down to the dock with a couple of beers in hand. He had to control himself as he took in Julie's long legs in those short cutoffs she loved to wear. At that thought, the riff from the ZZ top song “She’s got legs” ran through his mind and he muttered, “She sure does!”

“What was that, Aidan?” Julie asked.

“I said hey, what’s up?” Aidan replied.

“You are so the man of the hour,” declared Julie.

She watched as the flush spread from his neck up to his cheeks. It was one of the things that she found so endearing about him. Even though he had the looks which made all the girls stare and the athletic abilities to make the boys envious, he was still modest. All of that, and he was in the top five of his class academically year after year. *Admit it, girl, you love him. Yeah, yeah, so what’s new? Well, today I’m going to do something about it!* She thought to herself.

“What are you smiling about?” asked Aidan

“Oh, nothing, nothing,” Julie said.

“So, what do you want to do today?” he asked her.

“Well, since you asked, how about we go and socialize a little and then go for a swim?” she asked.

“That’s probably the best thing I have heard all day,” Aidan said

“Now, that I find hard to believe,” responded Julie. “I don’t think anything can compare to you winning today.”

“Well, that was a great feeling,” he confessed with a smile. “But it still comes in second to spending time with my friends on a beautiful day like this. Just hanging out and not worrying about anything, being able to relax and enjoy life. There’s also the fact that some of the girls here are pretty easy on the eyes.”

“Oh, really now?” she asked him. “And just who here has caught your eye?”

“Well, now that you mention it, those shorts you are wearing don’t look bad at all,” he told her with a lascivious grin.

“Oh, stop it!” she yelped, pushing him away so he would not see the blush that had just broken out on her cheeks.

With that said they walked to the crowd and were greeted by their friends, but as each went their separate ways, they kept looking at each other.

The conversation among the girls, to no surprise, was focused on the boys and who was dating who and who was seeing someone else on the side. It never failed that the conversation would turn to gossip and, as usual, Julie turned a deaf ear to it. She absolutely could not care less for the idle talk that most of her peers seemed to revel in.

"Julie, I have to ask. Are you going to finally make a move on Aidan or could I?" asked Theresa. Theresa was the prettiest girl in school. She was again, no surprise, the homecoming queen, a title she had won with ease. She was also Julie's best friend, and the only reason that she had not made a pass at Aidan was out of respect for Julie's feelings. She reminded Julie more frequently, though, that time was moving on for all of them and graduation was just around the corner. Then what? Well, Aidan would move on and if Julie was not going to do something, then Theresa would.

"Don't worry," replied Julie. "Today is the day that I finally let him know exactly how I feel about him. Then it's up to him what he does about it." She was terrified that she would be making a big fool out of herself, end up embarrassing herself and breaking her own heart on the mantle of "what could have been" for years to come.

Well, you only live once, she told herself.

Where is he? She spotted him talking with Jeff over by Jeff's Jeep. It was a big CJ that Jeff had spent a lot of time and money on. He had it lifted and on big tires; it looked good and sounded good too.

The way the light was hitting Aidan's face seemed to light him up with a glow that made him even more handsome, if that was even possible. The way that the wind was lightly ruffling his hair made her heart beat faster. Just then, Aidan looked right at her.

They had looked at each other like a million times before now, but nothing like this before. For some reason this was different, and they both felt it.

Aidan began to smile at her and then the smile kind of faltered. It looked like he felt the weight of the moment as well, one of those moments that you hear about, but never expect to experience. It felt as if she was falling into him, and the longer she looked at his piercing blue eyes, the more she let herself go with the feeling of falling. How long this lasted, she had no idea. It could have been a few seconds or maybe a few lifetimes. Time had become as irrelevant as the people around them. Nothing mattered besides the two of them. The spell was broken when someone passed in between them and broke their line of sight. It was as if they were both waking from a dream.

Julie made some weak attempts to re-engage in the girl-talk going on around her, but her heart wasn't in it. The next time she looked at Aidan he tilted his head towards the water and raised his left eyebrow. She loved how he did that.

With a smile on her face, Julie gave a small nod of her head. They didn't say much on the way to the dock. When they got there, Aidan simply asked, "Feel like a swim?"

"You just try to keep up!" Julie joked, not that it was much of a joke. She was a very good swimmer as well and could usually hold her own against Aidan over the short distances.

As they shed their clothes each of them stole glances at the other. The air was practically sparking with the unreleased energies between them.

Julie darted off like a sprite calling back, "Catch me if you can, big boy!"

Aidan didn't mind at all following her. It gave him a great vantage point to admire her well-defined legs pumping as she ran. Her legs went all the way up to her well-defined rear which, at the moment, was doing wonders inside her tight bikini bottom.

They were heading out to the diving barge that was in the middle of the lake. It was only about eighty yards from the shore, but that small distance kept most of the people away. In fact, at the moment, there was no one on the barge.

Aidan was looking forward to looking at her again as she climbed the ladder onto the barge, but these not so clean thoughts were shattered as he saw Julie go under the water.

This was not expected. She rarely swam underwater much-preferring freestyle.

"Aidan! Help! My leg is cramping." She called out to him as soon as her head broke the surface again.

Aidan gave a powerful kick and wrapped his arm around her waist then rolled her over. He easily backstroked their way to the safety of the barge. In-spite-of the searing pain in her right thigh, Julie couldn't help focusing on the not so insignificant bulge in Aidan's trunks. The sensation of feeling his strong arm around her and feeling his taut muscles working under her sent feelings racing through her young body.

They climbed onto the barge and collapsed on their backs catching their breath. They were more out of breath from their pent-up, mutual passions than from the exertion of the swim.

"Would you like me to massage your cramped leg?" Aidan asked.

"That sounds good," she replied

It wasn't the first time he'd massaged away a cramp in her leg. In fact, she knew he was good at massaging cramped muscles, and they both had given each other massages before. The difference was that this time the air seemed to be charged with electricity.

Before they knew what, they were doing, they were in each other's arms passionately kissing.

Julie eventually broke the kiss. With her head spinning, she looked into his eyes and said, "Give me a second to catch my breath."

Aidan quickly looked back to the shore to see if anyone was paying them any attention. Not that he cared if anyone knew that he had kissed Julie. He was just a person that liked to keep his business to himself. No one seemed to be looking at them.

"How's your leg?" he asked her.

"You really know how to take a girls mind off her troubles don't you, Aidan Thompson?" she replied playfully. "It really is feeling better. Help me stand up and test it a little."

He gently helped her to stand up. Supporting her a little at first as she tested her leg. He relished the feeling of her soft skin warmed by the heat of the sun.

"It seems to be okay but give me a minute to make sure." At that, she started doing some squats and flexing the muscle.

Aidan quietly admired her young body as she moved through the exercises.

"What do you say if we go over to that picnic area over there? It seems to be kind of secluded and, I don't know about you, but I wouldn't mind taking this a little further," she said to him as she looked right into his eyes.

"That sounds really good to me," he replied as he took her hand and walked to the edge of the barge.

She held him back for a second and said, "Please stay with me, Aidan. If I have another cramp, I want you there if I need you."

"Julie, I'll always be here if you need me," he told her solemnly. "I'll even be there when you don't need me."

They dove into the water holding hands.

As the sun was beginning to set, they rejoined their friends. They had walked around the lake attempting to be as discreet as possible on their return. During the walk, they had told each other just when it was that they realized they were in love. They talked about why they had not acted on it earlier and laughed together because they both had been afraid of being rejected and in fact had missed out on being together sooner. Aidan explained that it was her friendship above all else that he was afraid of losing; she was very special to him, and he did not want to risk losing her for anything.

Julie pulled him up short and cupped his face in her hands "You will never lose me. I love you."

"I love you too."

The rest of the night was one to remember. They sang songs around the campfire, roasted marshmallows, and ate hot dogs. It was clear to everyone that Aidan and Julie were now more than just friends, but this was a surprise to no one. In fact, most people asked them why they had waited so long. At this, they both only smiled and shrugged their shoulders.

Chapter 17

"I don't want to go Mom!" wailed Summer.

"I know, honey," replied Debbie. They had been going back and forth over whether Summer would go to the ballet recital, but Debbie knew from experience that this was nothing more than nerves talking.

Summer started last night, before dinner, complaining about her stomach feeling upset. Debbie knew enough about her daughter to surmise that it was nothing more than a weak attempt to get out of going to the recital. She also knew enough to watch for signs of Summer really having an upset stomach. It could be nothing more than nerves, but then again it was not unheard of for stage fright to cause real nausea. She also knew enough about teen girls to always be on the lookout for signs of an eating disorder. Summer had always had a healthy appetite, but she was growing up and was constantly facing pressure at school to fit in. Debbie wanted the best for her daughter and if that meant she had to keep her eye on her, well then, so be it!

Summer picked at her food at first but ended up eating a good amount before excusing herself and going to her room. Debbie went up a little later to find her sitting on the side of her bed and sat down next to her.

"Nervous about tomorrow?" asked Debbie.

"Maybe a little bit," mumbled Summer.

"A little?" Debbie let the question hang for a bit.

Finally, Summer opened up. "Mom I can't do it! I've tried and tried, and I still can't get it right! Here watch." Summer stood up and moved to the side of her room. She assumed a pose in the first position, executed her move and then, as she was crossing over, she stumbled. "See Mom? I can't do it! Every time I try, I make the same mistake. Everyone will notice, and I'll be so embarrassed." She sat down and started to cry out of frustration.

"You know, you may be right," Debbie said. "You may stumble, you might even fall down. Lord knows, it has happened before, and to ballerinas that are far more accomplished than you. Do you want to know what those prima ballerinas did when they fell down?"

A slight nod of a blond head of hair signaled that she was listening and wanted to hear the answer.

"Well honey, they got back up again and kept right on dancing. They kept dancing because that's what ballerinas do. They dance, baby! You're worrying so much about what might go wrong that you are making it happen."

"Look at me, sweetie."

Summer raised her eyes, so she was looking at her mom through her hair.

"No, pick your head up and look at me. There now, that's much better." Debbie reached over and put her hand on Summer's cheek. “Now hear what I have to tell you. Everyone falls down. It happens to all of us from time to time. It is going to happen. Accept that, and now move on from it. When it happens, smile a little, because that is one of those times that is then behind you. Pick yourself up, and dance. Don’t let fear hold you down.”

“You know how you feel when you are really into the dance? Remember the last recital when you danced to Swan Lake? I could see on your face that you were really into the dance. Do you remember how that felt? I remember there was a point where you really let go and just went with it. That’s what you need to do tomorrow, baby girl. Just let go and go with the dance. If you do that baby, you will do great.” Debbie put her arms around Summer and held her close to her.

After a few minutes Debbie sat up. “Now listen, I’m going to go back downstairs. Don’t practice too much. It’s more important that you get your rest. I’ll check on you again in a little while so don’t stay up too long,” Debbie said as she stood up from the bed and left Summer’s room.

Chapter 18

Debbie was putting the plates into the dishwasher when she looked at the clock.

"Hurry up, guys. I want to get there early enough for us to get good seats," she called out to the kids.

"Summer come on already!" Debbie called from the bottom of the stairs. She was tapping her nails on the banister.

"Alright, already! I'm here! Don't have a cow, will ya?" Summer complained as she came down the stairs, taking them two at a time. She could see the frustration written all over her mother's face.

"Stop right there, miss beautiful!" said Debbie.

"What now, Mom?" Summer asked, rolling her eyes as only a teen girl can do.

"Well, sweetie, before we go, I want to teach you a little technique I use when I'm really busy. Before I leave, I always pause and ask myself if I am forgetting anything. That gives me a chance to go over things in my mind before moving on to the next thing. It works for me. Why don't you give it a try?"

"Okay, if it means we can get going. Alright, now can we go Mom?"

"No," Debbie stated firmly. "Really try to use what I have just told you, please."

Seeing that she was not going to get out the door unless she did as her mom told her, she thought for a minute if she was forgetting anything. She retraced her steps quickly in her mind. Of course, she wasn't forgetting anything, she thought to herself. She went over what was in her bag. *Oh Crap!* At that, she felt a sensation on her shoulder. Her hand went up, and her fingers started searching for the strap of the bag that wasn't there. She was leaving her bag with her costume and ballet shoes!

She spun around and darted back up the stairs to her room.

Debbie smiled as she heard her daughter's feet pound back down the stairs.

Skidding from the bottom stair to slow down just enough to make the turn out the door, Summer called out, "Thanks, Mom! Let's go, or we'll be late!"

The door was already open, and she jumped into the van, over Aidan's legs.

"Hey, watch it, dweeb!" he called out.

"You watch it, daddy long legs!" she said right back at him.

"Both of you quit it already!" Debbie said as she got in behind the wheel.

As soon as they pulled up in front of the recital hall Summer called out from her open window, "Lisa! Wait for me!" She bolted from the van as soon as it had stopped rolling.

"Summer!" Debbie called out.

Summer stopped and looked back at her mom. She threw her hands up. "What Mom?"

"Remember baby, just relax and feel the dance," Debbie said to her.

Summer smiled. "Thanks, Mom," she said before turning abruptly on her heel and darting through the door after her friend.

Debbie and Aidan entered through the front door and were lucky to find seats right in the middle of the auditorium.

"Mom, do I still have time to go to the bathroom before it starts?" Aidan never wore a watch. He said he didn't need one and usually, he was right, most of the places he went to had clocks. He knew his regular schedule so well that he didn't need to consult a watch. When he did do something out of the ordinary, like this, he relied on someone else who invariably had a watch on.

"You still have about fifteen minutes before the recital begins," Debbie told him.

"I'll be back in plenty of time," he replied.

Aidan had been gone for a few minutes. She occupied herself by watching the people around her. The seats were filling up rapidly. The activity down by the stage was a barely controlled frenzy. Smaller children were running from their parents, up the stairs on the sides of the stage and behind the heavy black curtain that hid the backstage activity. Moms were busy putting the last-minute touches on hair and costumes. Further back from the stage families were settling into their seats. She was watching a family a couple of rows down, and over to the right, when she felt someone close to her, really close. She felt breath on the back of her neck and smelled her favorite cologne. She could tell from the voice that it wasn't Aidan. This voice was deeper and flirtatious.

"Hello, beautiful. Do you mind if I sit here?"

"I don't know," she replied turning to meet his direct gaze. "My husband may have a problem with me sitting next to such a handsome man."

"Well, he deserves it for leaving a beautiful woman like you alone for even a minute." Dave kissed her and sat down beside her, dropping the act. "I'm sorry that I had to go into the office today, honey."

"I understand, I'm just glad you were able to make it," Debbie told him. She held his hand and cuddled up to him.

"Where's Aidan?" asked Dave

"He had to go to the bathroom," Debbie told him.

Strange, thought Dave. He'd gone to the bathroom before coming down to sit next to Debbie, and Aidan hadn't been in there. Well, he may have been in one of the stalls he reasoned. With that, he turned his full attention on Debbie as they waited for the recital to begin.

Out in the lobby, Aidan was on the phone talking with Julie.

"I am sorry, Aidan, but I didn't feel well this morning. I didn't think much of it. My stomach's been a little sensitive for a week or so, anyway, while I was eating breakfast, I got sick. It was only oatmeal. I could understand if it was bacon and eggs, but it was plain oatmeal. I've been sick two more times since then," Julie told him. My stomachs settled down now, and I'm feeling a little better, but not much. I don't know what it is. I must have caught a bug.

"I'm so sorry that you don't feel well. Do you want me to come over? I can at least hold a cold towel to your forehead," Aidan offered.

"No, Aidan, you need to be there for Summer. I wish I could be there too," she said. Make sure you tell her how much I regret missing the recital. Have her call me when you get home, okay?" Julie said to him.

"Okay, honey," replied Aidan. "I love you."

"I know you do. I love you too, baby," she replied "Remember, call me when you get home, so I can congratulate Summer. I know she's going to do great!"

"Okay, I promise. Love you," said Aidan.

"Me too," replied Julie.

Aidan made his way through the darkened theater and took his seat as the curtain began to rise.

"Hey Dad, did everything go okay at the office?"

"Yeah, it did. Now quiet, the recital is starting. You do not want to upset a ballet audience, they can get really vicious. Remember, they don't eat as much as they should, so they are really angry." With that, they both laughed until Debbie told them both to shush.

Focus! Summer told herself. She was checking her ribbons before the curtain rose. *Remember, Dad is in the audience.* This was the first time he had made it to one of her recitals, and she wanted to do her best. She looked over and saw Anne and gave her a little smile. Summer could tell that the other girls were as nervous as she was. *Remember what mom said—Just relax and let the music flow.*

She took a deep breath and let the rising music wash over her. The curtain began to rise, and the dance began.

Dave could not believe what he was seeing. He had seen Summer's costume before, but somehow, under the lights, and with her fellow ballerinas, she was truly beautiful, all the girls were. The way that they were moving with the music, the lights changing color, it all created a magical experience that he had not anticipated. So, this was what he had been missing out on all the other times.

He had been missing out on so many things.

Summer wasn't nervous. She had let go and was just dancing. She was moving with ease, and then she looked at Tina Lemter. The look on the face of that girl was pure hatred. She saw her lips curl up in a wicked grin and then she mouthed, Oops! As they were crossing, she shot her elbow out.

The blow caught Summer in the ribs, knocking her off balance. The intense pain took her breath away. She stumbled a couple of steps before she regained control. Her concentration was broken. She struggled to get back into the rhythm. The dance was almost over by the time she recovered and was back in rhythm with the rest of the dancers.

As the curtains came down, she glared at Tina. Tina looked right back at her and blew her a kiss.

The gall of that bitch raged Summer. She held her temper in check throughout the rest of the performance. She had three more dances to perform. She tried to put it out of her mind and focus on the dance.

As soon as the encore bow was over, Summer turned and slapped Tina across her face.

No one was more shocked than Tina. Summer had always just taken the insults that she had subjected her to, and Tina never expected her to do anything about it, much less do anything physical.

Most of the girls had known about the bad blood between them. Those that hadn't seen Tina elbow Summer in the ribs had heard about it before the next song was over. The drama hung heavy in the air.

Ms. Gabby, the ballet teacher, had seen it all. While the other girls were changing out of their costumes, she called Tina and Summer to her office.

"You girls are both on your last warning. Tina, if Summer had fallen down, not only could she have been hurt, but up to five other girls could have then tripped over her. They could all have been really hurt. I don't even want to think about how bad it would have been for the show. Of course, it would have been ruined. Do you understand that Tina? You almost ruined everything!"

"And Summer," she said turning her glare on her. "Don't think I missed you slapping Tina. This is ballet, and I will not have you two make it into some back-street brawl!" Ms. Gabby did not raise her voice; she spoke clearly, and there was no mistaking the disapproval in her voice. "I will not let anyone make ballet an ugly spectacle. If you two can't work out whatever there is between you, then do not come back. I will not have you, or anyone else, ruin the dance. Both of you, get out of my sight before I kick you out of the class."

Summer went out to meet her parents with tears of frustration running down her cheeks. She would talk to Ms. Gabby another day and tell her everything, but for now, all she wanted to do was to get away.

"Honey, what's wrong?" Debbie asked when she saw her daughter.

"It's nothing, Mom. I really don't want to talk about it right now," Summer answered.

Knowing that the girls would talk about it later, Dave crushed Summer to him and lifted her off the ground and spun her around. "You were GREAT!" he exulted. "I never knew anyone could move like you did up on that stage! It was like you were one with the music. You were so beautiful! I'm so glad I came. I should have been coming to all of the other ones too. I just never knew what I was missing out on. You are great."

His never-ending praise brought a smile to her face in-spite-of her anger. She was so happy that she had made her dad proud of her. It really helped to get over the frustration of what Tina had done.

Summer tried to downplay how well she had done, but Dave wasn't having it.

"Look here," he said "I know that it takes a lot of courage to go onstage and perform like you just did. Not only perform but to do it well. All of the hard work and training that went into doing it. Do not minimize what you have done. It really is something you should be proud of. I know your mother, and I are. To show you just how proud we are of you, we are taking you and any of your friends that would like to come, to Happy Joe's Pizza and Ice Cream Parlor."

"Aw, Dad, that place is for kids!" Summer complained.

"Alright, then you don't have to come," Dave said casually. "But I would love to have a sundae with all of my favorite toppings before I watch them make my pizza and then eat enough pizza to make my eyes cross from being so stuffed." He puffed out his cheeks making it look as if he was about to burst. "Your decision though."

"Dad, you are so silly!" she said. With that, she ran off, and in no time at all, came back with twelve giggling girls, all talking at once. Thankfully, Debbie took over and ushered the young ladies backstage to get their things and make sure they had their parents' permission.

Aidan said goodbye and left with Dominick who had been there watching his kid sister as well. Dom's sister was a couple years younger than Summer but was showing promise, so she had been allowed to perform in this recital, despite her age.

Aidan and Dom decided to go over to see how Julie was doing. She answered the door looking tired in the face. Aidan was immediately concerned, but Julie told him to relax and go have fun. When he persisted, she told him that what she really wanted to do was to go to bed and rest for a while. As she closed her door, her mom came from the kitchen and leaned against the door frame.

"Is everything okay?" she asked her daughter.

"Yeah, I'm just feeling tired," Julie told her.

"No problem with you and Aidan?" she asked.

"No, Mom. Everything is fine except for this upset stomach I have."

"Okay baby. I'll make you some chicken noodle soup."

"Isn't that supposed to be for colds, Mom?" asked Julie.

"Well, that's what they say, but in my experience a good bowl of chicken noodle soup always makes me feel better," she said.

"Okay Mom, I'm going to lie down. Call me when it's ready, all right?"

"Okay, honey." When the soup was ready, she took it up to Julie, sat on the bed with her daughter and they simply talked. In the end, mother was right, the soup did help her to feel better. The talk they had helped even more.

Aidan saw the car parked out in front of Happy Joe's and came in to see what his family was up to. That, and he needed to borrow some money for gas. He congratulated Summer again and then went off with his friends, leaving Summer's friends talking about Aidan and his cute friends in his wake.

Debbie and Dave eased back and settled into their seats at the next table. Their ears really needed the break from all the high-pitched voices.

Debbie squeezed Dave's hand as she looked at Summer and said, "This is good."

Dave couldn't agree more.

Chapter 19

"Come on girl! Don't just let me take it from you. Work for it!"

"Okay, chick! Just remember you asked for it!" With that Summer dug in and brought up her reserves. The first half mile was history, and the next would decide the bet. In reality, the bet didn't matter. What mattered was that she won. It was something that she didn't tell others about. She was very humble and reserved most of the time, except when she was racing. When she was running, she was a force to be reckoned with. She was fast in the sprints, but not fast enough to be a real threat. In the mile and longer, though, she found her stride. She could run a 16:10 5K and then turn around and do it again. She loved to run. With the wind in her hair and a good burn in her legs, she was in her zone.

The petty problems of school, and that idiot Shawn Stephens, just faded away. At the thought of Shawn, she picked up her pace even more. Drawing even with Sandy, she flashed her a smile, and a wink then blew past her.

Damn! How does she do that? I'm going full out, and she blows by me as if we just started the race, Sandy wondered yet again. It wasn't like Sandy was a slow runner. In fact, she was ranked 4th in the District and had a personal best 5:05 in the mile.

It was a pleasure to watch Summer run, though. She had a natural rhythm and stride that made it look effortless. She was 5'8" and weighed in at 120 pounds of lean muscle. *Both she and her brother Aidan had inherited excellent genes*, she thought.

That Aidan sure is hot!

Don't get distracted now, Sandy chided herself as she noticed her pace had dropped off since Summer had passed her. *Dig in girl!* As usual, Summer was waiting for her friend at the finish line.

"Okay, that was good, Sandy. Shake it off and get your wind back. In two minutes, we go again. This time I pace you," Summer said.

This was their daily routine. A warm-up mile followed by three miles with one race and then each of them pacing the other followed by a cool down mile. Twice a week they followed this routine with wind sprints to work on their finishing kick. It was a good routine, and it was working.

They both had shaved time off of their personal bests and were ready for the meet against Jefferson High next week. Individually they both expected to do well in the mile and 3 mile, but in the mile relay, they expected to kill all challengers and set a new record. The other two girls that rounded out the relay team were solid, and Gomez had a finishing kick that really rocked.

Winded and feeling good about a good workout, the girls headed for the showers.

"So, what's the latest on the Shawn drama?" Summer asked. Sandy was the unofficial gossip queen at school and Summer regrettably wanted to hear the dirt on her ex.

That still didn't sound right. After all the time they'd been together, to have it all come crashing down only four days ago. Last Saturday night! She still got hot just thinking about it.

Shawn had brought her to Tanks house for a little get together, but one thing led to another, and they got into a fight.

Shawn had a beer, and when Summer told him not to have another one, he got upset.

"You are not alone, mister," she reminded him. "I want to get back home alive and drinking and driving is not the way to get that done. In fact, honey why don't we just go?" She asked him as she snuggled closer to him. "This party is just more of the same old stuff anyway." She tried to reason with him and diffuse the situation. She knew that Shawn could have a temper and lately he seemed to be ready to blow at the slightest thing.

"I'm getting tired of you always telling me what to do and when to do it," he said, not so much under his breath. Then he blew up. "Damn, Summer, why don't you just relax? It's only a beer! I've only had one, and another one is not going to make me pass out, okay?" With that, he stormed off.

Summer watched him for a little while as she talked with some of the girls at the party. She noticed Tina Lemter talking to him. Tina had a very loose reputation, and it was well deserved.

Summer knew that Tina wanted to add Shawn to her long list, but not while he was with Summer.

Summer hadn't forgotten Tina's elbow during the recital. Tina had not come back to the ballet class, but Summer didn't know if that was voluntary or if she had been told not to. In the end, she didn't care. As long as Tina Lemter was away from her, that was fine. But now, here Shawn was talking to her!

He knew about the bad blood between them. How could he even be thinking to talk with her?

Summer walked up to Shawn and took him by the hand. She tried to lead him away, so they could talk, but he shocked her when he jerked his hand from her. "I'm not going anywhere. You see that I'm talking with Tina here. I'll be with you in a little while." With that dismissal, he turned his back on Summer and resumed his conversation with Tina.

Summer didn't wait around to see what happened. She asked Tammy to take her home and tried in vain to keep the tears from flowing. She was more angry than anything else—how could he so easily dismiss her? After all the things they'd been through together.

"He said he loved me!" she wailed as she broke down and the sobs broke free from her aching heart.

Tammy pulled the car over to the side of the road. She turned down the radio and just sat there without trying to say anything. She was simply there for Summer.

As the wracking sobs eased Summer gradually realized where she was again. She looked over at Tammy and apologized for going loony on her.

"I'm usually not such a crybaby. In fact, I don't even know why I'm crying. I'm just so confused! How could he? How could he dismiss me so easily?" she wailed. "And for that tramp! Everyone knows what she's like. How could he choose her over me?"

Through all this Tammy just stayed silent. All she did was put her hand on Summer's shoulder.

The reassuring touch felt good; it felt steady and dependable. Right then it was what Summer needed more than anything. To feel something solid, as the mantle of her relationship with Shawn crumbled down around her. The faith and trust shattered by his dismissal of her.

After the tears eased up, Tammy listened to her as she blubbered about what she had lost and once Summer got it all out, Tammy looked her in the eye and asked kindly if she was okay to go home or if she wanted to go somewhere else.

Home sounded good. Summer could already imagine how good it was going to feel wrapping her comforter around her as she lay on her soft bed while crying her heart out for all time to come. Yeah, home sounded good. As they pulled up in front of Summer's house, Tammy took her hand and gave it a squeeze.

"Remember, you may feel that you are alone, but you're not. You have a lot of great friends. You are a great person, and this will pass. Believe me. If you need me, call me."

Summer thanked her, and once she was safely in her bed, she cried herself to sleep. She stayed in her bed all the next day and cried pretty much the whole time. She couldn't help it; the tears would not stop. It wasn't losing him that hurt so bad, although that did suck, it was the way that she had lost him. And to *her*! She might have felt a little better if he had chosen someone else over her, but to pick a girl that was such a total skank was more than she could bear.

No, that was not what was really hurting her. Total truth!

What really hurt more than anything else, what she kept on coming back to over and over again, was the way that he had just turned his back on her, turned away from her so easily.

That was what kept coming back to haunt her in her sleep, as well as what felt like every waking moment.

Monday was hell. As soon as she arrived at school, she could tell something more had happened by the way that she was getting looked at. It was just one of those things that you just know. The way people glanced and then quickly looked away. She knew there was a secret going around about her.

That changed as soon as Susan caught up with her.

"The story is that Shawn cheated on you with Tina, the tramp! What the hell is going on?"

"Well, I left him at the party at Tank's house. He was talking with her when I left," Summer replied.

"What? You left him while she had her claws in him, within your sight?" Susan asked, shaking her head.

"Hey, it wasn't like that!" Summer insisted. She then went on and told her the whole story. When she was done, Susan was furious. "I'm going to go and kick both of their asses."

Summer felt better knowing that her friend wanted to stick up for her. "Oh Susan, you are such a bobcat, but you know you're a great runner but not such a good fighter."

"This is so messed up!" Susan fumed.

"I don't care. It's over, and that's that," Summer said dismissively.

"Yeah, right sister. I hear you talking, but they are just words. I'll let you know what else I can find out. Gotta run!" Susan said as she took off down the hall.

Since that day, the only developments were that Shawn appeared to be depressed and wasn't talking with anyone, Tina the tramp, was talking to everyone, and all three of them were the topic of conversation in most groups in the halls.

For the thousandth time, Summer asked herself, *what if he didn't sleep with her? What if it's only a rumor? No, it doesn't matter!* She affirmed.

I need to go for a run! Instead of eating lunch she went to the track and, not even bothering to change into her sweats, she started running.

Running from her thoughts.

Running from her problems.

Running from the pain.

Running into the zone that she knew would soon envelop her in its soft embrace.

The rhythmic sound of her feet striking the ground taking her away from all her problems and toward whatever she would find.

Summer didn't know it, but she was being watched. A lone figure sat watching her run like she was being chased by the devil. It was fitting because Tammy knew that she was trying to exorcise the pain life had heaped upon her. The pain her friend was going through hurt her as well. If only she could take it away. Nobody could do that for her though.

It's something you have to go through on your own. I'll be there for you, girl. You're not alone, Tammy said to the wind.

In time things settled down. People found something else to talk about, and Summer was not the target of all the busy eyes; she was old news. The gossip machine had chewed her up and spat her out again.

Eventually, Shawn had even tried to apologize. He had left notes in her locker, called the house, and even tried to talk to Susan to get to her. That was not a good idea on his part. Susan shot him down so hard he was probably still stinging over it; she had a very sharp tongue on her when she wanted. No bluster at all, just cold hard truth right between the eyes and she let him have it with both barrels.

Shawn denied doing anything more than ditching Summer and trying to make her jealous. The real problem, he said, was that he was frustrated that they had not taken their relationship to the next level, so he was only trying to make her jealous. What a crock of bull! The truth was that he was angry, so he wanted to make her angry too. Well, he had achieved his goal. She was furious about so many things, and they were all about Shawn! She was angry that she had believed he really cared about her; angry about the way that he had simply dismissed her as if she was some piece of trash to be thrown away, angry that he could think that he could blame his actions on her making him wait to go all the way with her; and, on top of all of that, she was angry at herself because she still loved him. Loved him but would never go back to him. Never would she allow anyone to treat her that way again.

Tammy had turned out to be a rock for her. She was so patient and understanding, she really knew how to listen and, just as importantly, not to judge her. She could tell her anything. That was it right there, Tammy was someone she could trust. Wow, it was surprising how good it felt to realize that about someone.

Okay, sister time to focus on what's important and that's the meet at Franklin in a couple of days. Time to dig in and run like the wind. Use the pain to fuel you. Use the hurt to push you along. Use the anger to stoke the fires!

Now run!

And that's what Summer did. She ran, and she ran well. The meet at Franklin saw her setting two new state records and three school records. They shattered the state and school records in the mile relay by six whole seconds. She only continued to improve from there.

She had running, she had her friends, and she had her family. Eventually, the pain of losing Shawn faded away.

Chapter 20

The hospital cafeteria was never empty, but at four in the morning, it was as close to empty as it ever got. Debbie was sitting there half listening to the seemingly never-ending problems that Lisa had to deal with. Chief among those were her husbands' shortcomings. According to Lisa, her husband was not interested in her anymore, and she thought he had to have someone on the side.

As much as Debbie didn't want to pass judgment on anyone else's struggles, it was apparent to her that Lisa was, at least to some extent, responsible for her own situation. According to her story, long and tediously rife with details as it was, she would criticize her husband for even the smallest mistakes. She would jump on him if he was even a little bit late coming home from work. Debbie could easily imagine the pressure he must feel to perform in the bedroom. It really was no surprise to Debbie that more-often-than-not he decided to forego what minimal pleasure he could have enjoyed in favor of not suffering through the inevitable assessment of his shortcomings, in this most intimate of engagements. He chose instead to not rise to the temptation.

"So, you see, it has to be another woman? Right, Debbie? I mean look at me. I'm still hot, right?"

Yeah right, thought Debbie as she nodded her head enthusiastically. Lisa wasn't ugly, but she sure had not been focusing on fitness lately either. "Every woman looks into a broken mirror." She had no idea who said that, but it was definitely true. Every woman's view of herself was distorted, one way or the other. She either saw what she feared to see, or she saw the lie she wanted to believe. In this case, it was the latter. She refused to believe that she had gained weight. Debbie thought it likely that if her poor husband even suggested a salad or going for a walk, he had to endure a scathing diatribe about his failures, whether they were based on the truth or not.

Debbie tuned out the Lisa show and focused on her own life drama. She couldn't judge anyone too harshly. Lord knows, she had enough problems in her own life. She would be the last one to cast a rock in a glass house such as hers.

Her relationship with Dave had continued to cool. Dave had focused on cutting back his time at the office and, to be fair, she had to give him credit for that. He was also spending more time with the kids. In many ways, things were going much better since the weekend at the lake. Dave was making an effort, but Debbie could not muster up the energy to meet him halfway. When she was really honest with herself—and she couldn't imagine telling anyone else this—she just did not feel like trying anymore. She was tired of trying. She was tired of working for it. Shouldn't it just feel right? It used to feel right! It used to feel so right that she built her whole life on it.

Debbie knew that it had been the right choice. Dave was the man she loved. But was he *still* the man she was *in love* with?

She had gone around and round with that one. Was she being selfish for even thinking that she needed that kind of silly schoolgirl passion at this point in her life? Should she hope for such blind love? Was it just that life had jaded her from appreciating the real love she had with Dave? Was she just being a stupid fool?

All these questions and more had raced around each other in her mind.

"So, tell me, do you think I am being a stupid idiot or is he having an affair?"

The look on Lisa's face told Debbie that she sincerely wanted an answer. What should she tell her?

"First of all, I don't believe that he's having an affair."

With the look of relief that washed over her friend's face, Debbie knew that she had to quantify her statement, and quickly, or else all would be lost.

"I don't think he's cheating on you, but I think that he may be close to doing something. Remember Lisa, I don't know your husband, so this is only me talking about what I think of human nature, okay?"

With a slow nod of Lisa's head that set her short bobbed brown hair in motion around her chubby cheeks, Debbie continued.

"I think that he may just be under a lot of pressure. You said it yourself, the economy is tight, and you guys talk about just barely making ends meet. Think for a minute about how that must make him feel. You know how it makes you feel, right? Well, he probably feels the same pressure to provide for the family."

Debbie went on in that vein, trying to make Lisa realize that her husband was in the same place as her and the extra pressure she was putting on him was not helping their situation. She could only hope that Lisa listened to her.

How much of her own advice should she take home with her? Debbie wondered if she had become selfish in her own way.

I suppose I have. Or maybe I am just getting older and wiser. Maybe I just don't have to put up with things like I did before. Why should I put up with something if I don't feel like it? She held this internal debate with herself as Lisa went on with her own external debate.

Debbie had become very adept at going through the motions lately. She did so now. She nodded her head at the appropriate times and only vaguely registered that the flow of the external and internal conversations soon began to mirror each other. On a very distant level, she acknowledged that both she and Dave were responsible for how things had become.

Wait a minute. She snapped more into the here and now. She realized that she was wrong. Dave had been making an effort, and she had been the one simply going through the motions. She had not really been trying to re-solidify their relationship. Lately, she had to fight stronger and stronger to resist the urge to pull away from him when he reached out to her.

Debbie let her eyes drift around the nearly empty cafeteria. She saw that most of the people that were here when she had arrived had already left. She checked her watch and saw that her break was supposed to have been over 10 minutes ago.

Lisa thanked her for the advice and promised to keep her updated. Debbie smiled and hoped she at least tried to ease up on her husband.

On the walk back up to her ward, Debbie let her mind roam where it would. It kept coming back to the point that Dave was trying, and she was only going through the motions. She needed to make a decision. Things could not go on like this for much longer.

“Hello, Nurse Thompson. I’m glad you’re back. I need a hand with the patient in 327.”

“Yes, Doctor Andersen, what is it?”

As Debbie listened to what she needed to do, she couldn’t help her mind from wandering a little. It never failed—every time she was close to Doctor Andersen, she felt attracted to him. It wasn’t like anything was going to come of it, but he was a good-looking man. She stopped herself from that attempt at justification. It was more than his looks, and she knew it. She was attracted to him on many levels. He was smart, successful, yes good looking, but most of all she really liked the way he handled himself. He had an easy confidence about him.

When they were done with the patient in 327, they continued together for the rest of Dr. Andersen's rounds. They did work well together.

"Well, Mrs. Atkins that about takes care of it," said Dr. Andersen as he held her hand. "Remember that you have to take your IV stand with you."

"I hate the thing," she told him. "It makes me feel like I am on a leash."

Mrs. Atkins was still feisty at 92. She was a very independent woman and let everyone know it.

"I understand, but we talked about this, you need the medicine and the fluids."

"I know, but that doesn't mean I have to like the damn thing."

He gave her hand a reassuring squeeze and watched Debbie finish taping off the IV catheter.

"Okay Mrs. Atkins, we're done here. Try to get some rest. If the test results continue to improve, we may be able to release you tomorrow."

Debbie followed him out of the room and into the hall. Instead of turning back to the nurses' station he turned right. "Buy you a cup of coffee?"

"No, thank you. My shift is about to end, and I am going straight to bed. I'm dead on my feet."

"You look fresh as a daisy," he said with a big smile.

"Doc, you really need to get your eyes checked." She smiled in spite of herself.

"Well, how about I buy you breakfast? That way you don't need to worry about it when you get home. You can go right to sleep."

"Okay, I am a little hungry. Meet you in the caf in half an hour?"

"Sounds good Debbie, see you then."

Chapter 21

Dave was surprised to see Aidan standing in the driveway. Instead of pulling in he parked on the street.

"Hi son, how was your day," he asked, as he got out of the car.

"It was okay, Dad. Do you want to shoot some hoops?"

"Yeah, that sounds like fun."

Dave put down his satchel and draped his suit jacket over it. When he stood up, Aidan passed him the ball. Dave dribbled the ball a couple of times and then rose up for a jump shot. The ball gracefully arched its way to a perfect ... air ball!

Aidan couldn't hold the laugh back.

"Okay, so I need to warm up a little," Dave said with a smile.

Aidan shot a jump shot of his own and was rewarded with nothing but net.

"Nice shot, son. Let's see if I can do better this time."

Father and son fell into the rhythm of the game and soon lost track of time.

Debbie came home and parked behind Dave's car. She sat there for a minute and watched the game. They were pretty evenly matched and were both working hard to gain an advantage. She could see the signs of Dave's effort; his dress shirt was soaked with his sweat.

Aidan saw her first. He had just scored an easy lay-up.

"Hey, Mom, do you want to play?"

"I think I'll pass. It looks like you boys are enjoying yourselves. Who's winning?"

"I'm up by four."

"Not for long, young buck!" declared Dave.

"We'll see about that."

"I'll leave you boys to it," said Debbie as she went into the house.

Aidan made another easy jump-shot.

"Your shot is really improving. Have you been working on it?" asked Dave.

"A little. I come out here and just shoot around. Summer joins me sometimes too. Dad, do you think mom will have to keep working these long shifts for much longer?"

"I don't know, I hope not. She said it's because of reduced staffing. Hopefully, they will hire more people soon."

Dave took advantage of Aidan's distraction and stole the ball from him and scored a lay-up of his own.

"Oh, you know that wasn't right!" complained Aidan

"You know you gotta keep your eye on the ball, son."

"Oh really? So that's how it is, huh?" Aidan reached out and stripped the ball from his father's hands. To add insult to injury, he dribbled around him and then faked left then drove right and scored another lay-up.

Dave saw that real soon these lay-ups were going to become dunks. Aidan only had about another inch to go before he could slam it in.

When Summer came home, she joined in. Dave played a little bit more, but it soon became apparent that he was doing more watching than playing. He retrieved the ball from the yard and used the chance to bow out and watch his kids play. He was surprised to see how good Summer was. She had a pretty good game. She was fast and was really good on defense. Aidan had four inches on her in height, but she didn't back down. In time, Debbie told them all to come in and get cleaned up for dinner.

"So, tell me, Dad, have you got your breath back? You seemed to be pretty well out of it while we were playing."

"I was a bit winded, I'll admit."

"A bit winded, he says. Mom, you should have heard him. He sounded like he was going to collapse."

To her credit, Debbie just smiled and kept her pretty mouth firmly closed on the subject.

Dave didn't miss the look in her eyes. That look that said she knew how out of shape he still was.

"Okay, enough about me, Aidan go wash up. It looks like Summer already beat you to the shower."

Dave took the opportunity and went to put his arms around Debbie. She stopped him with a raised spatula. "Don't come any closer to me with that sweaty shirt, mister."

"Come on, honey. You used to like it when I was all sweaty."

"I mean it, one more step and I *will* swat you."

"Now that's more like it!" he said as he leaned in a bit closer.

Debbie backed up a step.

"Just kidding, honey," Dave turned away and went to take a shower himself.

Once he was out of the room, Debbie let out a long sigh and let down the façade. Her shoulders drooped, and her head hung low as she turned back to the stove.

"I can't keep doing this," she said to herself and the pork chops, shaking her head. "Something has to give."

She remembered clearly when her life had become so complicated. It was a Wednesday night, and she decided to stop off at Geno's to grab a pizza for her and the kids. Dave had told her that he had to work late on a big project. Nights like this were now the exception, instead of the norm, since he'd been making an effort to trim his hours down.

She'd been waiting for her order when she saw Jake Anderson turn around with his pizza in hand. It was just a chance meeting, and the surprise of their encounter was plain on both of their faces.

She noticed that he had a small size pizza and she smiled as their eyes met.

"So, you found the best pizza in town," he said to her. "Do you come here often?"

They both laughed at what sounded like a corny pickup line, and once the thought flashed through her mind, she had to fight to keep from blushing.

"No, not really. I was just grabbing something quick to bring home to the kids for dinner. How about you?" she asked.

"Same here, with the exception of the kids' part. Just grabbing a quick dinner to go. Well, buon appetito," he said.

That brought a smile to her face as she watched him go. She heard her number called and went to the counter to pick up her order.

On her way back to her car she noticed Jake sitting behind the wheel of his truck talking on the phone.

She found herself wondering who he was talking with.

Okay, girl, stop it right there! She chided herself. *You are a married woman with a husband and kids. They still need you.*

That was a sobering thought. *Need me? Well yeah, the kids do, but does Dave?* For so long he had made work his focus. Now that he was making an effort to focus on the family, she was having a hard time adjusting. She was confused about how she felt towards him.

Just as she reached her car the tears of frustration began to flow. All the time that had gone by, all the years that she had adjusted to him not being there had made her used to him being gone. The fact was, that now that he was in her life more physically, she still felt that he was gone. She still felt that there was that separation between them, and she was starting to worry if too much time had passed. She was afraid that her marriage was ending. She felt a big emptiness facing her, and that scared her.

To make matters even more confusing, she really missed him. She missed that closeness they used to share. She just felt empty. Dave was there, but still not there. She was the one that was keeping him away.

At that, she broke down completely and let the grief wash over her. Grief was what it was too. She slowly felt her Dave slipping away from her. No matter how hard she fought herself to keep the feelings of love for him alive the harder it became. True, before the weekend at her parents she had not exactly felt close to him, but she still loved him. Now, there was love but, it was changing as time went by.

She was startled by a gentle tap at her window. As she looked up, she recognized it was Jake. He was looking at her with concern written on his face. She rolled down her window and wiped the tears from her cheeks knowing that her makeup had to be a mess.

"I'm sorry if I startled you," he said, "but I saw you walk to your car, and then when you didn't drive away ... well, I just wanted to see if you were okay."

"Thank you, Jake," she said, "but, as you can see, I am not completely okay right now. I just had a small emotional breakdown, but the worst of it has passed."

"Do you want to talk about it?" he asked.

She surprised herself by doing just that. Over the next twenty minutes she talked with him, and, to his credit, Jake did not interrupt her rambling narrative. When she was done, all he said was- "It sounds like you have been doing quite remarkable, everything considered."

"Yeah, that's me," she said. "A little wonder woman."

"No, really," Jake said, "you were basically running the whole household while your husband was focused on his job. You were running the house and juggling your very stressful duties at the hospital. Which, I must say, you do very well. You are very good at what you do and have a smile for your patients and your children even though you are dealing with all of these hardships. You are doing fantastic with what life has dealt you. Anytime you need someone to talk with please feel free to come to me."

"Thank you," she said. "I really needed to get that off my chest. I'm sorry that I made your dinner cold."

"Don't worry about it. That's what microwaves are for."

With that, they said their good nights, and she watched him drive away, not knowing anything more about what it was that he went home to. She was grateful he had been there for her tonight.

She decided to go back in and order another pizza. She wanted the kids to think she was doing okay. If she got home and needed to warm the pizza up again, they might worry about her. They had enough things to worry about in their lives. She didn't need to add anything more.

That night at Gino's had laid the groundwork for a relationship that built upon itself. Debbie found herself looking forward to having lunch and or dinner with Jake at the hospital. She enjoyed talking with him. Since that night she'd found out that he had been married but had lost his wife to a fight with ovarian cancer four years ago. He had moved back to town to care for his mother who was getting on in years and did not want to go to a care center. Actually, he said that he liked the shift to a smaller town; he had lived in Sacramento since completing his internship and was happy to return home. He said that he liked the slower pace and felt that he was making a real difference here, admitting that in Sacramento he had felt that he was just processing patients and not taking care of them. He feared that had he stayed there much longer he would have started to see them as cases and not people. He liked being able to take the time and talk with his patients, to interact with them. He felt that he was really making a difference and that was why he had been interested in becoming a doctor in the first place. Debbie could relate with him on that. It was the reason she had been interested in becoming a nurse.

Yes, Debbie knew that the problem was not with Dave. It was with her. She had changed.

With dinner ready, she called her family to the table.

Chapter 22

A distant rhythmic beeping was coming from somewhere. Dave felt like he was floating. It was not a free sensation, it was more like a feeling of being disconnected. He tried to reach out his hand to grab onto something, but everything felt sluggish like he was moving through water. His searching fingers did not find anything to grasp. There was no sensation of movement. He was just ... there.

Where am I?" he wondered.

He began to hear faint voices. They seemed to be coming from far away, but he couldn't fix on what direction they were coming from. He strained to hear what they were saying. He could tell they were voices, but the sound was too soft to make out what they were saying. Whatever they were saying was not important to him though. He felt extremely tired. He had never felt so exhausted, tired to his bones and needing to rest. A weight heavier than the universe was pulling him under again.

"Doctor, will he be okay?" asked a nurse with a concerned look on her face.

"We've done all we can for him. His head injury was the worst of it, but aside from some short-term memory loss, he should recover fully. It was probably the cold temperature of the water that saved his life in the end. We don't know how long he was in the water for, but it had to have been a while. It's a miracle that he's alive at all."

"Does he know about his family?" she asked him.

"Nurse Fran let's talk about that out in the hall," said the doctor in a kind voice. "You know they say that there have been cases where patients can still hear even if they are otherwise non-responsive."

The voices faded away as the nurse's shoes squeaked down the hallway.

Dave struggled to pull himself out of this nightmare. No matter how hard he fought, he could not get away. He could feel himself being pulled under again.

"All right, kids let's be quiet," Debbie told them. They were in the hall outside of the door to their dad's room. "You know daddy needs his rest to heal. We can only stay a short time." Debbie had tried to prepare them before going in to see their dad, but she knew that no matter how much she said, seeing him lying in a coma in the hospital was going to be a shock. There was no way around it though. Their dad was in there, and they needed to come to terms with that. Hopefully, it would not be for long. *God, I hope it's not for long. I don't know how I am going to manage without you, Dave!* She thought to herself once again.

“Don’t cry, Summer,” Debbie said. “Daddy will be okay. You know how strong he is right?”

“Yes Mommy, it ... it's just that he looks like he’s in pain. Mommy, do you think Daddy would like me to tell him a Scary story? You remember right? He used to tell me the stories before bed.”

Debbie remembered the stories very well. Summer had asked him for a scary story when she was two years old, right after Halloween. So, Dave made up a story that started out sounding scary but was filled with happy characters and her own family. They both loved the Scary stories, and they evolved over the years until Summer eventually outgrew them in favor of more accomplished tales. On this day, however, she needed a return to those innocent times.

“Honey, I think Daddy would love for you to tell him a story,” Debbie told her daughter. Debbie put her hand on the side of her beautiful daughter’s face and looked into her upturned eyes. She nodded her head slowly and said, “Go ahead, honey.”

So, with that Summer began, “It was a dark, dark night and Scary was walking down a trail in the forest. She heard a sound in the tree. Oooh, what’s that?”

At the end of the story, Summer was sitting by the side of the bed, holding her dad’s hand. Debbie would never forget the look on her daughter’s face. It was a lost look that would haunt her.

“Mom?” she asked.

"Yes, honey," Debbie replied.

"Is Daddy really sleeping or is he somewhere else?"

"Honey, I really don't know," Debbie answered.

"I want to think that he is only sleeping, but Mom, I'm scared. At times I feel like he's not here." Summer started crying as her Mom held her to her side. Summer was still holding onto her Dad's hand, and they stayed like that until Summer's tears stopped. Then they stayed in the room for a while longer.

"Aidan, do you want to say anything to your Dad? You haven't said anything since we came here." Debbie could tell that her son was seriously thinking about it.

"Mom, I don't think that he's ready to listen yet," Aidan said finally, looking at the floor. "I feel that he knows we are here. I can almost feel him being here and then it's like he slips away. Maybe it's only my imagination playing tricks on me. I really don't know. I do know that I don't feel like talking with him like that yet. I look at him lying there and think of him sleeping, but I can't help but remember when I was little, and I would sneak into your room. Dad would always wake up. Somehow, he always knew that I was there, and now ... well, he just doesn't."

When he finished talking, he looked up into his mother's face and asked her if she knew what he meant.

"Yeah, honey I guess I do," Debbie replied "I just feel that he is here and listening to us. You may be right that at times he is farther away. But I have to think that he is here."

Aidan looked her full in the face and then nodded his head slowly one time.

With that said they all grew quiet and retreated into their own thoughts.

A little while later Debbie took a deep breath and asked: "Are you guys ready to go?"

Without saying anything more, they stood up. Summer gave her Dad's hand a squeeze before letting it go. Aidan gave his Dad's shoulder a squeeze and knelt down to whisper in his ear.

"Dad, I don't know if you can hear me, but I love you and want you to come back. We all miss you. I want you to know that I will do my best to look after mom and Summer until you come home. You just get better, Dad. I love you." With that said Aidan stood up and walked out into the hall.

Debbie bent down and gave Dave a long kiss on his dry lips.

"I miss you, baby," she told him. "Come back to me!" Debbie gently closed the door behind her as she walked away.

Dave struggled to pull himself out of the nightmare. He tried to swim to the surface, but no matter how hard he swam, he never seemed to move. He kicked his legs harder but seemed to go nowhere. He thrashed his arms down, and suddenly there was something to push against. He saw a faint light and moved toward it. The surface was rushing up to him.

"Dave, wake up! Wake Up! You're having a bad dream."

He opened his eyes and saw Debbie looking down at him.

“Are you okay? That must have been some dream! Look what you did to the sheets.”

Dave looked down and saw that the bed was a mess. The sheets were tangled around his legs and wrapped around his waist. He must have really been struggling.

“What were you dreaming about?”

Dave told her about the nightmare. He couldn’t express his true feeling of being trapped in the dream, the feeling of being powerless. The feeling of being pulled down. It was too intense to put into words. The dream was already fading from him. Fading even as his skin was still clammy with the cold sweat.

Once he had calmed down Debbie lay back down and was soon fast asleep, but Dave was wide awake. The dream had really shaken him up. He could not calm down and relax. He felt, more than anything, a sense of loss. He turned his head and looked at the profile of his sleeping wife. She was lying right there and might as well have been a million miles away. The gulf that lay between them had continued to grow. At this late hour and with his wife lying right beside him, Dave felt that he was all alone.

Chapter 23

It was early on a Saturday afternoon, and Dave was clicking through the channels on the TV. Nothing held his attention for long. He felt like doing something instead of just sitting around in the house on such a bright sunny day. He turned off the TV and sat forward on the couch.

"What do I want to do?" he asked himself.

Aidan was out, probably spending time with Julie, and Summer was over at a friend's house. Debbie would be at work for another couple of hours. "Well, I guess it's just me and all of my friends," Dave joked with himself.

He made up his mind and got up off of the couch. He was going to surprise Debbie with a warm meal when she came home. He was already thinking about what he needed to buy as he went to put on his shoes.

Having finished with shopping at the grocery store, Dave was driving home, not thinking about anything in particular. As he was waiting for the stoplight to change, he looked over and realized where he was. Across the intersection was a restaurant that he had not been to in years, a little Thai place that he and Debbie had ducked into to get out of the rain one afternoon. The food had been good, but a bit spicy so they hadn't gone back again. He noticed that a woman sitting in the restaurant looked familiar. With a start, Dave realized that the woman was Debbie. Right there at the table by the window, she was sitting with another man.

The light had changed without him realizing it. Dave was startled from his daze when the car behind him honked the horn. He eased his car across the intersection, his attention split between driving and watching the scene play out at the window table. Dave was stunned to realize that his wife of 17 years was holding this stranger's hand. There was no mistaking what was right in front of his eyes.

He turned his head and forced himself to focus on the road before he got into an accident.

"Another accident!"

That foreign thought startled him as much as the sight of his wife holding the other man's hand. Where the hell had that thought come from? He had never been in an accident in his life.

Dave shook his head in frustration and gripped the steering wheel tighter. He needed to focus on one thing at a time. He reached out his hand to change the channel on the radio but stopped before he reached it. His hand was shaking. Dave realized that he was also breathing fast. He had to get control of himself. First of all, he needed to go someplace where he could park the car and think. He focused on his hands as they gripped the steering wheel, seeing that his knuckles were white from the strain of how hard he was squeezing it. He forced himself to relax his hands, then he reached out and turned off the radio.

He needed to get his head straight and decide what to do.

"What *do* I need to do?"

He made up his mind and took the next right, pulling into the city park. He needed time to go over what had just happened. His head was throbbing from all of the jumbled-up thoughts that were tumbling through his mind. His mind was racing so fast that it was impossible to think clearly. Thoughts whizzed through, one after another so fast that he could not work it out. He needed to gain some perspective, he needed to think this through.

"Maybe I should just go back there and punch the guy's lights out."

He could see the scene it would cause in the restaurant and knew that he would probably get arrested. In the end, the only thing that it would accomplish would be to further distance Debbie and give him a criminal record. As tempting as punching him was, it would not solve the problem. "Why was Debbie in the restaurant with him in the first place?"

He kept seeing her face. She'd had that little smile that made her eyes crinkle at the corners. He loved to look at her like that. Well, not when she was looking into another man's face and holding his hand!

He slapped his hand down on the seat as hard as he could. The stinging pain in his hand felt good.

He had pulled the car over at a spot that was kind of secluded. He got out and walked over to the picnic table and just sat down, shell-shocked. He had never imagined Debbie having an affair. She was a beautiful woman, yes, and their relationship had grown distant, but still—it couldn't have really come to this?

He heard the birds singing their songs to each other, completely oblivious to the fact that his whole world had changed. He watched as a squirrel scampered across the ground in search of scraps left behind.

That's what this felt like, scraps left behind. What was left? Oh God, what was left?

He sat there staring at nothing at all.

Then fits of sobbing wracked his body, and he raged at the sky.

In the end, an answer came to him. It was simple really. He loved his wife and didn't want to lose her.

He was going to do everything he could to win her back.

He was not going to mention what he saw. Instead, he decided to focus on what he could do instead of what may or may not be going on. In the end, he may lose her, but he decided that he was not going to do so without a fight. And the best way he saw to fight this was to make her fall in love with him again, if that was still possible.

Chapter 24

As Debbie was walking up to the door, she smelled something good wafting on the air. Her first thought was that one of the neighbors was going to have a good meal, but then she noticed it was the smell of her favorite meal. The aroma of roasted lamb and potatoes assailed her senses as she pushed open the door to her home. Setting her purse on the entry table she saw that the dining room table had been set and candles were placed all around the dining room. She could hear Dave humming to himself in the kitchen. She hung her coat up in the closet and went into the kitchen.

"You must be feeling better today," she said.

"I am," Dave answered. "In fact, I am feeling better than I have in a long time. I went out and did some grocery shopping. I really appreciate all the hard work you and the kids have been doing around here and I want to do more to help out. Even if it is something as small as going grocery shopping. I admit that I was a bit lost. It has been a long time since I have been in a grocery store, but I managed okay."

"Is there anything I can do to help?" she asked him.

"Sure, I got some wine for us and some soda for the kids. Could you set them on the table? The salad is ready, and the main course will be done in five minutes. You just have time to slip into something comfy before I call the kids down. How was your day?" he asked her as he kneeled down to look in the oven.

That caught her off guard.

"Okay" she responded Not only could she not remember the last time he had asked her that question, but today of all days, it made her feel guilty all over again.

She climbed the stairs in a daze thinking about the events which had led her to today.

It was three months ago, and she was having lunch with Jake. Like usual, the hospital cafeteria was busy, and they shared the table with six other people. Before long the other people finished up and left.

Jake surprised her by asking her to go away with him for the weekend.

"I'm not pushing, mind you, but it would be good for you to get away and relax for a while. I have a little sailboat that I'm taking out for the Labor Day weekend and would love for you to come along. There are three cabins aboard so don't think I am talking about an illicit weekend tryst. Although I think by now you know how I feel about you, I also think you know I respect your situation and your marriage. Debbie, I am not pushing you at all, but the invitation is open. I'm leaving Friday morning at eight and would love for you to come along. Think about it and let me know." With that, he got up and walked away. Debbie was stunned. She didn't know what to think but decided to not think about it until later that night, after work, after the kids were settled in bed. *Yes, I'll think about it then,* she told herself.

Despite that honorable promise, she found herself able to think of nothing else. Not only for the rest of the day but every waking moment leading up to Thursday night. She was so torn over the offer that she hadn't been able to sleep except in fits and starts.

In the end, she decided not to go. It would only complicate matters, and they were complicated enough. She worked through the weekend and tried to avoid Jake at the hospital. She didn't feel comfortable looking at him after rejecting his offer. That was why she was surprised to find a picture of him in her locker. The picture was of him standing on his boat with a smile on his face. Written on the back were the words 'I miss you.'

She had kept that picture in memory of the weekend she could have had. She knew where things would have led had she gone with him on the boat. She wanted it very much; she was more than attracted to Jake. She felt an easy bond with him on more than just the physical level. Not that there was anything wrong with his physical level. He was handsome and was in great shape. But, more than that, she was at ease with him. She found herself laughing a lot more when he was around. He made her feel good, and she needed that.

In spite of all that, or maybe because of it, she resolved that she wasn't ready to complicate things. She wasn't ready to give up on her marriage.

As the weeks went by, she also found out that she was not ready to give up on Jake. It was crazy, but she really missed him. She missed the way she felt around him, she missed their easy relationship. They still saw each other, and as life so often does, it grew ever more complicated.

As time passed, they found their way again. Their easy banter returned, and Debbie felt better about things. He truly was a great man.

Debbie had arranged to meet with Jake at the Thai House to talk with him. She resolved to lay it all out on the table.

She felt very nervous and had a small drink of wine to calm her nerves.

"Jake, you have always been honest and forthright with me. I owe you as much."

Jake sat forward and focused his full attention on her.

God, this is hard! I don't want to hurt him, but there is no other way. "You know how special you are to me. No, I am sorry, that is not complete honesty. You know that I love you." Jake's whole face lit up with his smile and, unable to help it, Debbie smiled too. Just as quickly as it arrived, the smile fell from her lips. "I love you Jake, but we have to end this." She raised her eyes and looked directly into his. "I am not going to leave my husband. As much as I want to be with you, I can't leave my family behind. I won't hurt them like that. They deserve better from me." As she said that last line her eyes focused on her hands. She reached across the table and held his hands in hers. "You deserve better too."

The conversation went on for a while, but Jake understood and, as usual, was very supportive.

She told him that she had decided to put all of her efforts into her marriage and bringing it back from the brink. She looked him in the eye and told him that she would always wonder what it could have been like, but she did not want to mislead him into thinking there was any chance for the two of them.

Earlier in the day, Debbie had gone in to talk to her boss and asked to take a couple of weeks off. She explained a little about her situation as an explanation for no advance notice. Her boss told her that she understood and gave her the time.

These things flashed through her mind as she went into her room to slip into something comfortable as Dave had asked. If only she could slip into the same comfort with Dave, she felt when she was with Jake. Well, that was what she was going to work on.

She retrieved the picture of Jake she had kept in a hidden place. She turned it over to read the words he had written there. "I'll miss you too," she whispered to herself and then put the picture away. With that, she closed off a part of her heart and opened the door to another.

She decided to not only change into more comfortable clothes but to also freshen up her makeup and perfume. Not too much, just enough to look decent. She could tell that Dave noticed by the way he looked at her as she set the drinks on the table.

Chapter 25

Dinner went very well, and it felt great to be sitting together as a family again. The kids were very animated throughout the meal sharing what was going on with them.

"I'm going to swim in both the 100 and 200 breast-stroke as well as the relay," Aidan said as he stuffed his mouth full of mashed potatoes.

"The swim meet is Saturday, Dad. Will you be able to come?"

"I wouldn't miss it for the world," Dave told him. He reached over the table and held Debbie's hand.

Debbie was surprised and looked up into Dave's smiling face. She was able to manage a weak smile and squeezed his hand back. She resisted the urge to let his hand go. *I have to hold on.*

"I have a recital in three weeks," said Summer. "Will you be able to make that too?"

They both assured her that they would be there for her too.

"Does anyone have room for dessert?" Dave pushed back his chair and went into the kitchen. When he came back, he was carrying a steaming apple pie. Now, this was surprising because for all of the time Debbie had known her husband he had never once baked anything. It was delicious!

After dinner, they all settled down to watch a movie together. Debbie cuddled up to Dave like the old days.

As she did so, he wondered briefly about what he saw earlier in the day. Immediately he pushed the thoughts out of his mind. He had made up his mind that he was going to concentrate on his marriage and everything else just did not matter.

He held her close to him and breathed in the smell of her hair. He had forgotten how good it was to be this close to her, to simply hold her.

The movie ended, and the kids went up to bed. Debbie went up to tuck them in. When she returned, she picked out a romantic comedy and put it on.

She settled back in beside Dave and watched the movie. After a little while, she sat up and snaked her arm across his shoulders. She looked him in the eye before leaning in kissing him. She snuggled her head into the crook of his neck. It felt good to be this close, this comfortable again. She turned her had and began kissing his neck. She slowly started to kiss her way down to his chest. His breathing became shorter and shorter. She took his hand and stood up off of the couch, pulling him after her and led the way up the stairs, past the pictures on the wall of a happy family as it grew. He noticed that the pictures stopped with Summer's 9th-grade picture. He hesitated and almost tripped. *That couldn't be right. Why would there be such a gap?*

Before he could think about it anymore, Debbie tugged his hand, and he went after his wife.

They continued the cuddling they had started on the couch but didn't take it any further. They were both content to have come at least this much closer.

Debbie could hear Dave's steady breathing. She knew he was asleep. She had lain there for what seemed a couple of hours, her mind running in circles. Try as she might she could not find rest. She turned her pillow over. The other side had become wet with her tears.

In time sleep took her into its embrace. If she had any dreams, they were no more relaxed than she had been when she finally drifted off.

"So how are you doing today?" Dave heard the voice. It was comforting and familiar though he could not readily place it.

"Okay, I see you still want to act the part of the strong silent type," she said to him as she wiped his chin, cheeks, and neck. Dave could feel the warm cloth as it caressed his chin. He could feel the texture of the cloth as it was rubbed on his chin with a confident and efficient touch. It was not sensual in nature, yet it was comforting.

"It's okay, I like it when a man knows how to listen," she said to him as she moved down to his arms. She proceeded to not only clean them but also to massage the muscles with her strong, practiced hands.

Dave could feel everything and hear her talking with him, yet he could not open his eyes. Strangely, this did not cause him any fear. He let it go for now. He didn't fight his lethargy.

"Too many men today think they need to talk and talk and talk. They talk about how they feel and try to impress you with what they think they know. I prefer men that are smart enough to know when to talk and then say the right thing. More importantly, though, I like it when a man simply knows when to shut up and listen. Not necessarily to me, but just listen, you know?"

"It's okay, honey. I know when you are ready you will talk my ear off. I suppose you are still waiting for the right opening."

Strong, confident hands massaged the muscles in his calves. They kneaded the withered muscles underneath the thin, dry skin as they worked their way confidently down his legs.

"That's okay by me, honey. You take your time," she told him. "It's a nice day today. Do you want to go outside and sit in the sun?" She didn't expect him to answer her. He never had after all these years that she had been looking after him.

"It's okay, honey, you just rest, and Chantal will take good care of you."

Dave woke with a scream locked in his throat. He was breathing hard and was drenched in a cold, clammy sweat. His heart was beating so hard it felt like it was trying to come right out of his chest. He sat up and frantically looked around, expecting to see the walls of a hospital. Instead, he saw that he was in his own bed at home. Yet, he could clearly smell the antiseptic in the air. There seemed to be a squeaking sound fading away. It sounded a lot like a nurse's shoe on the hospital's worn tiled floor.

He shook his head to clear it. It was as if the separation between the land of dreams and reality was nothing but a thin membrane. He squeezed his eyes shut and rubbed them with his fists. He was afraid that when he opened them again, he would be back in his nightmare.

His eyes shot open when he felt a hand grip his shoulder. He violently twisted away from the touch.

"Dave, wake up! You were having a bad dream."

Debbie had woken up to find Dave sitting up in bed. She became immediately concerned when she saw the state of fear, he was in. He was looking at something that had scared him terribly. Whatever nightmare he had jumped from it had been a bad one.

"I had a terrible dream. I was in a hospital. Instead of being in a bed I was in a wheel chair, and this woman was taking care of me. She was cleaning me. Like, giving me a sponge bath, and talking with me as if I had been there a long time. I can't begin to tell you the sense of being trapped inside myself as I listened to her talk. I wasn't able to respond to her.

"I wanted to tell her that I didn't belong there, that I belonged here with you, but I couldn't do anything but listen to her. I could actually feel her washing my face and arms. When she told me that it was a nice day and asked me if I wanted to go outside for a while, I swear I could actually feel the warm sun on my face. Debbie, it was all so vivid! I guess that's what scares me the most, it felt so damn real!"

"That's okay, baby, you're here with me now. You don't need to worry about going back there again. I am with you now."

Debbie put her arms around her husband and pulled him into her. She lay back against the headboard and cradled his head against her chest, running her fingers through his hair. "You are safe now. Just relax and go back to sleep. Everything is going to be okay, I promise." The reassuring sound of his wife's voice took away his terror like nothing else could.

He turned his head and looked up into Debbie's beautiful face. There was enough light coming in through the window for him to clearly see her. He stared into her beautiful green eyes.

Debbie broke the contact and looked away. She turned her face up toward the ceiling and took a deep breath. "It'll be okay, Dave. I'm not going anywhere. I'm right here."

Dave didn't see the tear slide down her cheek. He couldn't know the awful feeling of loss, that overcame her, when she told him that she wasn't going anywhere. By saying that, she was affirming to herself that she wasn't leaving him. She was also affirming that she wasn't going to live her life with Jake.

She was never going to feel Jake in her arms like this. She was letting him go, and holding on to her husband, her family. It was the right thing to do. But it didn't make it any easier.

Chapter 26

Dave had a meeting with his boss, and they talked about what had been going on in the department over lunch. The company was doing well with the ongoing market recovery and was actually gaining some market share on the competition.

Dave had another reason for this meeting beyond reviewing the performance of his department.

"Jim, I've been thinking that it's time for a change. I want to form a separate research division. With the company growing, it is taking more time to run these discrepancies to ground. I want to take three of my people to get it going."

"Did I hear you right, Dave? You want to lead this new division? Do you have a replacement in mind for accounting?"

"Susan Johnston is my choice. She's been with the company for almost as long as I have, and she's been my assistant for the past six years. She knows the job as well as I do."

In fact, it was one of the rules Dave had as a leader. He taught all supervisors the lesson that he had learned from an old Master Chief on his first ship. That Master Chief took the time to pass on his wisdom to Dave when he had been onboard for only two months. He asked Dave: "How do you know when you are a good leader?" Well, back then, Dave had no idea, and he told the Master Chief so.

"You know you are a good leader when you can be gone, and everything goes on as if you are there." He explained further that it was a leader's job to train his people to work at the same level of knowledge that he was working from. "Bring your people up to where you are, and they will carry you to success."

Over the years Dave spent a lot of time pondering those wise words. He went over them from every angle and to this day had never found any errors in that crafty Master Chief's logic. As Dave applied those simple rules throughout his career, they became a central part of his leadership style.

He had given a lot of thought to this shift in structure. One of the main reasons was the resolution he had made to himself to delegate the responsibilities of the job as much as possible. His decision to completely invest himself in his marriage and family was also a big reason for the change.

"I'll be there for Susan whenever she needs me. I will be able to focus more attention on conducting causative research and getting to the bottom of the discrepancies. By focusing on this area my team will become more efficient and hopefully be able to catch the problems sooner."

With that part of the meeting complete, it was time for the next item on his agenda. "Jim, I need to take a couple of weeks off."

"Is everything okay? It isn't like you to take two weeks."

"To be honest, no Jim, things are not okay. I mean they are, but I want them to be better. I want to spend some real time with my family. I have been neglecting them and want to focus more on them."

"I think that is a very good idea, Dave."

Chapter 27

Debbie and Dave decided to look into going someplace. The kids were in school, so they couldn't take the time off, but Dave figured that Aidan was old enough to take care of things while they were gone. They decided to go to a travel agency and see what last minute specials they had and found a ten-day getaway to Greece.

The island of Crete was a perfect place for them—they both loved the ocean, and the coast provided some great spots for both scuba and snorkeling. Whenever they needed a rest from the water, the beaches were some of the best they had seen. The fine sand and the crystal-clear water were stunning. At night the quaint town by day turned into a bustling hub of activity. Strolling along the port area the flow of people was surprising. Restaurants lined the harbor with waiters standing in front of their restaurants calling out their specials. They were remarkable to watch. They would fluently shift from one language to the other depending on where they thought the tourist was from. Dave heard one go from Spanish to Italian to English before he settled into German, all within the time it took them to pass the forty-foot space in front of the tables he was trying to fill. From the look of things, he was doing a good job because there were only two tables Dave saw which were vacant.

The couple made one loop of the waterfront and settled on his restaurant, and surprisingly he acted as if he remembered them. Dave was sure that it was a good sales tactic he used instead of a remarkable memory. Then again, he had flipped through four languages without missing a beat—maybe he was that good.

The food was delicious, and they thoroughly enjoyed themselves. The sound of the water lapping in the harbor mixed with the low murmur of conversation reinforced the intimate setting.

Dave was glad to see that Debbie was enjoying herself. She was sitting back in her cushioned chair and was savoring her glass of merlot. As busy as the place was, the staff made no effort to move them along.

Dave sat forward and took a piece of bread from the basket. He poured some olive oil on it and savored the taste.

"So, lovely lady, what would you like to do next?"

"What do you think if we just walk around a little?"

"Whatever the lady desires. I am at your beck and call."

"My beck and call, huh? I could get used to that."

Dave sat up surprised. Debbie had taken off her shoe and was rubbing her foot against his leg.

"You should see the look on your face, big boy," she said with a beautiful smile on her face.

They watched the flow of the tourists going by for a little while longer, then they drifted along the current themselves until they found themselves walking along a small side street. To call it a street was being generous—it was barely wide enough for a car to pass through. The souvenir places were still open. With their display stands out and the tourists walking, it was quite crowded. They meandered along and picked up some things for the kids.

Their wanderings brought them to another small side road where the crowds were a little thinner. Dave looked to his left and saw a bar with a part of the wall glowing in a calming blue light.

"Hey honey, want to go inside for a drink? I know I could use one."

Debbie had been busy browsing through a display of silk scarves. She looked over her shoulder and was ready to tell him no. She wanted to shop some more. When she saw the place, she changed her mind. The blue light made the bar look very comforting.

"You know, that does sound like a good idea. This place looks cool."

"Yeah, it does, doesn't it? Come on," he said as he took her hand and led her inside.

The door opened, so they were looking at the calming glowing wall. They realized that it was an even better effect than they had realized. Water was cascading down the face of the wall, and the combined effect of the light and the sound of water was very soothing. They turned their attention to the bar, pleased to see that the front of the bar had plastic strips that ran its length which was alight with calming hues which changed colors. The décor was modern but warm. The top of the bar was a dark wood and, as Dave looked around, he was pleased to see that the tables were the same color of wood, as were the shelves above the bar that held the liquor bottles on display. The barmaid was a beautiful blonde. She greeted them with a smile and asked them in English what they would like.

"This place is beautiful," said Debbie. "I love the effect of the falling water."

"When I first started working here, I thought it would drive me crazy. That was three years ago, and I still like it. It's so relaxing," she said with a far-off look in her eyes. She looked at Dave and Debbie, bringing herself back to the here and now, and said, "So what will it be?"

"Well, since this place looks so nice it puts me in the mood for something fancy. Do you have a recommendation?"

"I think I have something that you will like." She went to work making a tall glass with lots of bright colors in it.

She slid the exotic looking drink in front of Debbie.

"What's it called?" Debbie asked, before bending forward and taking her first tentative taste. "That's really good. I mean really, really good."

"I am glad you like it. I call it Tingly Toes."

"With a name like that there has to be a story behind it."

"Not really, it's more of a subtle warning. I have found that the more of the drinks you have, the more your toes tingle. Well, they do until you can't feel them anymore," she said and then started laughing. "Seriously, they are pretty strong."

Dave was not as adventurous as Debbie. "Do you have any single malt scotch?"

"Would you like it neat or on the rocks?"

"On the rocks, please."

They took their drinks to one of the tables by the window and settled in to watch the crowds walk by. After a few minutes, the bartender asked them if they would like to go upstairs. "This is mostly a local's place, but I think you two will fit in nicely."

Dave raised his eyebrows in a questioning look.

"There is nothing strange to be worried about. We just like things nice and calm here. A lot of the tourists that come in are loud and a bit rude," she explained. "There are places on the waterfront that I refer them to. Those places have loud music and loud patrons. It's a perfect fit for them. We like to have a nice fit here too. I really think you will like it."

"Okay," said Debbie. She took her drink in one hand and led Dave up the stairs

The person that designed this place really knew what they were doing, thought Debbie as they walked up the stairs. The railing was the same wood as the bar. The changing light effect was on each side of the stairs lighting the way in changing hues. When they reached the top, they saw that the bar up here was larger and took up the center of the room. Throughout the room leather couches were arranged in groups of three.

The place was not very busy with only maybe 20 people, mostly lounging around on the couches. It was not even at half capacity. There were some small groups, but most of the customers were couples. The place had a very intimate feeling. The music was at a low comfortable level. It was not so loud that you had to shout but still loud enough to cover casual conversation.

"Dave, I think that the lovely bartender downstairs was a very honest person."

Not knowing where this was going or where it was coming from Dave just looked at his wife and smiled.

"My toes are definitely tingling. It is kind of funny, but so is the tip of my nose." Debbie's eyes were crossed as she looked at the tip of her nose.

Laughing, Dave reached across and tried to extract the drink from Debbie's hand.

"Oh no you don't, mister! I didn't say that I minded my toes and my nose tingling."

They both broke out into a fit of laughter.

When she had finished her drink, they made their way out of the bar. Dave noticed how wobbly her gait had become, so he put his arm around her and pulled her close. They stopped along the way to thank the bartender that had greeted them.

"You are the perfect person for this place. You are beautiful like the rest of this place and are just as welcoming," said Debbie. She was rewarded with a big smile from the young lady.

"That is very sweet of you. I hope you had a good time."

"We did, and I have to tell you that you were right about that drink. My toes and my nose are tingling."

The bartender smiled and said, "Come closer. Can I share a secret with you?"

"Of course, I can keep a secret."

"Well, just between us girls," she raised her eyes up to Dave and gave him a wink, "it has been known to make other things tingle too."

Debbie leaned back with a shocked look on her face and put her hand over her mouth before she broke down into a fit of laughter.

The lovely bartender was laughing along with her.

"You two are a lovely couple," she told them as Dave supported and guided the still laughing Debbie towards the exit.

As they passed the water cascading down the illuminated fall, Debbie reached out her hand and ran it through the water. She surprised Dave by wiping the water across his forehead.

She was not quite ready to go back to the hotel, so they made their way toward the waterfront. They walked with their arms wrapped around each other's waist, strolling down the same path they had taken earlier. The crowds had thinned out some, but the restaurants still had most of the tables occupied.

The music from the other side of the harbor had risen in volume. It seemed that the nightclub scene was getting going. They were heading towards the lighthouse at the end of the wharf. Vendors were on the side of the walkway trying to hawk their wares. They ended up picking up a hand-crafted bracelet for Summer and a yo-yo that had a picture of the harbor. It looked like the picture was taken from where they were currently standing and looking back towards the restaurants. They both thought it was a cool souvenir.

They sat down on the wharf beside the old lighthouse, their feet dangling over the side, well above the waterline. Off in the distance, they could see the lights of a ship as it made its way on the dark waters.

"What kind of boat do you think it is?"

"It is a pretty big merchant ship. Probably one of them container transport ships. Look, you can tell because, do you see that red light?" Dave asked as he pointed his finger in the direction of the ship. He then moved his finger to the side a little. "And do you see that smaller light there, just behind it?"

"Yeah, I see it."

"Okay, that is the stern light. Now, look there." He said as he moved his finger a little to the left. "Do you see that light?"

"No, where is it?"

Dave reached over and put his arm around her and pulled her closer to him. He reached his arm out and pointed to the light. "You can see it if you strain a little. It is not very big, but it is there. You can tell it is one of those big transporters because of how far it is in front of the red light. The red light is on the bridge wing on the side of the ship. On one of those ships, the bridge is toward the back of the ship. That is the reason for the one white light being so close to the red light. The other light is farther away because it is at the front of the ship. That ship is really big, and the front is really far from the bridge."

They sat like that for a while watching the boats navigating the dark waters. After a little bit, Dave noticed that the flow of people had trickled down to only a few. He looked over and saw the vendors packing up their wares.

"Are you ready to go, hon?"

Debbie nodded her head in answer. Dave stood and then helped her up, deciding it was time to call it a night.

Later that night, they were lying in bed and listening to the cicadas play their symphony. The orchestra was backed up by the accompanying percussion section of the surf breaking on the cliffs outside of their windows. There was a cool sea breeze that was coming in their room to cool off the heat of the day.

Dave was surprised when Debbie rolled onto her side and looked at him. She had her head resting on her arm. Her hand began to twirl his hair.

"That drink was perfect," she said. "My nose is still tingling."

The smile came easily to Dave's face. He loved it when Debbie was happy. Maybe it was the alcohol talking, but she sounded like she was really happy.

"In fact, it is not just my nose that is tingling."

"Oh, are your toes still at it too?"

"Well yes, but that was not what I was thinking about."

Dave looked over at her. "So, what were you thinking about?"

Debbie rolled on top of her husband. "How about if I just show you?" She silenced any more questions as she kissed him. The little kisses soon gave way to deeper ones.

Maybe it was the alcohol. Maybe it was because they were on vacation. Maybe it was a combination of all of it. In the end, Dave didn't care. Their bodies fell into a natural rhythm. They heard the sound of the tide as it crashed against the rocks less than one hundred feet away. Their passions crashed over them. Sometime later they drifted off to sleep, holding each other's hand, to what now sounded like the gentle surf.

One evening, they decided to be a bit adventurous and asked their hotel manager George for a suggestion on where to go.

He recommended a new disco that had opened recently, and everyone said was a lot of fun. They told the cab driver the address for the disco and set off on their adventure. They were beginning to get a bit nervous. The taxi had been driving for at least twenty minutes since they had pulled out of town and Dave began to wonder if they were being taken for a ride, and not in a good way either.

He had heard stories of people being taken out into the country and then charged high rates just to take them back home.

His fears proved to be unfounded as they approached a building that had cars lining both sides of the street. There was definitely something going on ahead of them.

He tipped the taxi driver and asked him to come back to pick them up again in three hours. The taxi driver happily agreed.

The pathway to the disco was beautiful, Dave noticed as he listened to the click of Debbie's heels on the concrete sidewalk. Small palm trees lined the walk-way, and they had what looked like Christmas lights wrapped around their trunks illuminating them. The entrance itself had the velvet rope and standard guards barring access. There was no line of people waiting, and Dave wondered if this place was a good idea or not. The guards didn't give them any problems as they strolled right past them—they either didn't look like trouble makers, or they were there to handle the line if a crowd was to form.

Once they were inside, they were able to better understand what was going on.

The entrance area was done up to look like it was carved out of a cave. The lighting was dim, and the sound of falling water could be clearly heard as they walked past a large rock that had water cascading down its craggy face. The rock, or more appropriately boulder, sat in the center of the entranceway. The walkway was about thirty feet wide, and just past the boulder they were cast in a black light. Dave looked over at Debbie, and they both mugged big corny bright white smiles at each other.

The disco itself was set up in one main room, and there were nine other themed rooms off of it. Three levels circled the main room which was easily the size of two football fields. Circling the room were the walkways that threaded their way up and around the main room. The other themes were techno, retro, and others they did not immediately recognize. The only constant was that they were loud and busy. Inside the main room, laser lights were shooting through the air. Dave could feel the bass beat of euro-pop as it pulsed its rhythm through his body. The crowd was not thick, but, then again, it was still early. It was only eleven, and they had come to learn that things did not really get going until at least midnight.

They bought some drinks and set off to explore the place. To say it was big was saying nothing. They explored a few of the rooms and danced a little; the house room was fun. Everyone was jumping up and down more or less in time with the beat. They soon realized that they did not need to know how to dance to blend in. All they had to do was jump up and down and wave their arms in the air.

That was fun for a little while, but they decided to move on and see what else the place had to offer. The next room was a surprise, Country music with a techno edge was booming from the speakers. Some groups were doing a passable two-step. It was fun, and Debbie surprised Dave by how well she could two-step. He tried to remember if they had ever gone out to a country bar. He couldn't recall ever going there with her. He decided it was probably best that he not ask how she had become so good at country dancing. It was probably something she had learned in high school anyway.

After a few songs, they had enough and moved on to the next theme. It was a retro room. They found music from the 60s and 70s, but with a twist. The beats were euro-pop and some of the ladies were dressed up like they were from the 60s with longer skirts. The guys were wearing suits and ties of the time. Others were dressed like flower children with peace signs and flowers in their hair.

They took a break from their explorations and rested on a couch that was off to the side and away from the pulsing music and crowds of dancers. The lighting was soft and gave them a feeling of isolation. Once their eyes adjusted to the dark, they realized they were not alone. Other couples were making use of the secluded area as well. Sounds were coming from the back that told them that at least one couple was making full use of the couch they had. They realized that something had changed.

The dull roar of the crowd was different.

They stood up and walked over to the wooden rail to see what was going on.

Looking down on the crowd below, they were surprised to find that the crowd was looking up at them. No, not at them, they were looking at something above their heads. They followed their gaze up and saw that the massive ceiling was separating. It was retracting in upon itself to reveal a sky filled with stars. This alone made the trip out here worthwhile. Then the laser light show began. The lights pulsed to the beat of songs that they didn't recognize but loved anyway.

The show went on for quite a while. After the initial awe of the spectacle had worn off the crowd went back to dancing, or in the case of some, jumping up and down. Dave and Debbie made their way down to the main floor and joined the dancers. They were soon moving along with the crowd dancing to the throbbing pulse of the music, a mass of humanity moving in time to the rhythmic beats.

Debbie called his attention to two men that had appeared on each side of the main floor. Each of them was holding a large tube. The crowd raised their hands in the air and started yelling and jumping with even more energy.

Dave didn't know what to expect, but they were caught up in the moment and followed along with the crowd. Soon they were covered in white foam. They smiled at each other and decided to just go with it.

The music was pulsing, and the crowd was feeding off of each other's energy. Dave didn't have any idea how long they had been out on the floor dancing. The songs blended together with only the smallest differences in the beat. There was fast, and then there was faster.

Eventually, they both decided they had had enough and walked outside to see if, by any chance, their taxi driver had returned for them. They were in no hurry and enjoyed walking back out arm in arm. They agreed that if he wasn't there, then the club could always call a taxi for them, but they were pleasantly surprised to find out that their taxi was waiting for them.

Their driver's name was George, and he told them he had coincidentally just dropped off another couple at the club and luckily was able to pick them up. Dave thought that was very likely, but he also thought that he would have come back for them anyway. It was a Thursday night, and he didn't think business was brisk enough for him to turn away a paying fare.

"So, did you guys have a nice time?" asked George.

"It was a wonderful place," said Debbie "I am sure you have heard this before, but the ceiling opens up to the stars, and they have a laser light show. It was so nice." Debbie leaned into Dave and gripped his hand.

"We plan on doing some shopping tomorrow. Are there any places you would recommend?" Dave asked him. He went on to tell George what kind of things they were looking to buy.

George was very helpful. He gave them directions to a good area, saying that while they had the typical things tourists were looking for, they also had some interesting local wares as well. They thanked him for taking such good care of them and wished him and his wife and eight children well. George then revealed that one of his many talents was the gift of prophecy.

"You two are going to stay married forever. I know this is true. It is foretold. I am an expert in these matters. Hey look, I have been married for 32 years, with 8 children and 11 grandchildren. On top of that, I have all of this experience watching people as they climb in and out of this cab."

Dave reasoned that so far, George the wise had proven to be correct. They decided to take his advice and see what they could find for their souvenirs.

The next morning, they left the hotel early after having eaten a light breakfast of croissants, yogurt, and drinking a passable coffee while listening to the sound of the sea breaking on the rocks of the coast on the southern side of the island.

They spent the morning strolling down quaint alleyways looking at the wares offered, leisurely browsing among the typical tourist items. The handcrafted chess sets on display were truly works of art. They were crafted from crystal, obsidian, or jade and in so many different forms that it was simply amazing. Debbie picked up a few pieces of porcelain with historical Greek themes hand painted on them and marveled at the workmanship that went into making them.

They bought the pre-requisite number of postcards, and simply enjoyed spending time together, in such an exotic location. The sounds of the merchants haggling with the customers, and among each other, mixed with the smells of the meat shops that were along every street they came upon, created a sense of adventure. There was also the feeling that you get when you are in a place that has been around for a very long time. People had been doing the same thing as Dave and Debbie were doing for thousands of years, in this same place. Eventually, their meandering path brought them to a leather shop that had belts and wallets on display outside of the store. The smell of leather permeated the air. It was obvious that the quality of the merchandise was very good. Debbie came up to Dave with a gleam in her eye and a satchel clutched in her hand.

"Dave, this is just the thing you need. That old one you have looks like it's ready to fall apart." Seeing the look that had shadowed his face, she recovered quickly. "Stop right there, mister! I am not offending your faithful companion, Satchel. It's not his fault that he's in the condition he's in. He has served you honorably and faithfully. It's not his fault that you took advantage of him. He did his best to accommodate the ever-increasing burden you placed on him. You literally worked him to death."

"Seriously Dave, it's time to replace it, and this one looks really nice. In fact, it looks a lot like your ever-trusty companion only a little bit bigger. Just think, it can actually hold more." She gave him a big kiss which sealed the deal. Yes, the good times were what it was all about!

They spent the afternoon at the beach, snorkeling and sunning. It was incredible, but it was already their last day on the island. They decided to try an authentic Greek restaurant.

They found a nice place that was recommended by a couple of the souvenir vendors. The place looked clean and had a quiet atmosphere. They explained to their waiter that they wanted to sample some Greek food. He was happy to oblige.

While they were waiting for their meal to arrive, they snacked on fresh bread with fresh olive oil. The waiter surprised them by bringing them each a shot of Ouzo. He had brought one for himself as well.

"Stin Ighia Soo! Cheers!"

They followed his lead as he threw back the drink. Dave and Debbie were both surprised by the effect of the shot.

"That sure took my breath away," declared Dave.

Debbie was still taking small breaths.

"Are you okay, honey?"

"I will be. That was a bit more than I expected," she said as she looked up at the smiling waiter.

"It is good, yes? Ouzo is Greek. Greek is strong. You will get used to it. You will like it, yes." With that, the smiling waiter went away to tend to some other business.

Dave and Debbie both hurriedly took a bit of bread in the hope of tamping down the fire in their bellies.

Later that evening, with the sound of the surf and the cicadas, they relaxed and soon found themselves in each other's arms. They tried to take their time, but passion flared and ignited a long-dormant lust that neither of them could resist. They rode the crest of their pent-up emotions until she collapsed on top of him breathing hard. They stayed like that for quite some time, simply enjoying being as one.

"What are you doing?" Dave asked her with a playful tone of voice.

"You're not getting off that easy, big boy," she said while slowly moving her hips. She felt him rise to her urgings and picked up the rhythm matching her rising tide of passion. Her slow rhythmic movements had the desired effect on him. She could tell that he was more than up for another round and they both took it slower this time.

They cried out from their pent-up passions. It felt so good and so comfortable to be back together like this again. This time he collapsed on the bed next to her as they held hands with their legs intertwined.

The only words spoken were his as he said: “I’ve missed you so much.”

Her response was simple and eloquent as she rolled into him and put her head on his chest. They fell asleep like that, wrapped in each other.

Before she drifted off Debbie lay still, listening to her husband’s steady breathing.

So, I’m not alone in that either. All this time I’ve been suffering with these feelings of being alone. I never stopped to think that he felt the same. I always thought that he was so busy with work that he didn’t miss me. I thought that I was only an abstract concept to him. Kind of tied in somewhere with the kids and house. Not even a real person anymore. Well, I guess I was wrong. He has missed me, and he still loves me.

In that moment she let go of Jake in her heart and gave herself to her husband and re-committed herself to him.

No reservations. No doubts. Nothing but this oneness.

Chapter 28

Things settled into a routine yet again, but there was a new dynamic at work this time around. Both Dave and Debbie were focusing on each other, they were paying attention to the little things. Dave was pleasantly surprised to find himself checking the clock in his office more frequently. Now he was looking forward to the end of the workday because he was going home to his family.

He had been able to expand the job of causative research in the months since returning from their vacation. He had added four more people to dig into the trails left behind, as the company expanded not only in market-share but also throughout the Midwest.

Dave made sure to keep work and home life balanced. He was determined that he was not going to fall into the same trap he had been in before. Life was going well.

Things at home were also coming along nicely. They kept working on their relationship. It was not all roasted lamb dinners. They had their share of arguments as well, but the difference was that they were talking with each other. When they did get upset with each other, they talked about it afterward. They didn't just brood over it and go off into their shells. They apologized to each other when one, or both would lose their cool.

They were both focused on making their marriage work, and it was great. The kids were doing well in school and sports, and Debbie and Dave both made it a point to take each of the kids for some special mom and/or dad time.

Chapter 29

Dave was driving down a winding road in the mountains. The feeling of dread was increasing; he knew something bad was up ahead. He didn't want to go to that place, but he knew he had no choice in the matter. The closer he was getting to the curve, the more he felt like turning around and just going home again.

Why do I need to go back there again? he asked himself. He had no ready answer but knew he had to.

Before that fateful curve, there was a clear area off to the side of the road. He pulled the car over and parked. He sat there, gripping the steering wheel in his hands for a little while. He did not want to get out of the car. He knew, if he did, he would go there.

He found himself opening the door, almost against his will. He knew that he had to do this and realized that nothing was going to stop him. His destination was only about two hundred yards away, but it felt like a million miles.

His feet felt heavier and heavier with each step. He now knew that he was stuck in a nightmare. He could clearly hear the crunch of the gravel under his feet. The air was still. Not a sound of traffic disturbed the peaceful morning. The birds were singing, but they were far away, their sound muffled. The stillness was comforting. He was overcome with a strong desire to go back to his car. All he wanted to do was to just turn around and go home.

What will this accomplish? It won't fix anything. The only thing you will find out here are more questions and self-criticisms, he told himself. In-spite-of this, or maybe because of it, he willed himself to keep going.

On a deeper level, he knew he needed to face this place again. He didn't know why, or what he should be expecting to find, but he was not turning away.

The curve in the road looked completely unremarkable. He realized that he had stopped walking and was just standing there, his eyes focused on a pair of skid marks that ended at the edge of the road. He had no idea how long he'd been there when he shook his head, trying to clear it. He was compelled to look over the edge. He didn't want to, but he knew he had to none-the-less. He peered down the side of the mountain. From up here he couldn't tell if the stream at the bottom was raging or quiet. His mind filled in the blank. He felt the icy waters rushing past. The icy embrace stole his breath away. He felt the ache all through his being from all the way up here.

Dave just sat on the edge of the guardrail for a while. He noticed the strange looks on the faces of the few drivers as they passed by. They probably thought he was crazy sitting here. Oh well, let them think what they would. He hadn't come here for them. He was here for a different reason.

"I thought I might find you here."

Dave looked up and saw a glowing woman walking towards him. As he stared in disbelief, Debbie materialized from the illusion. The sun behind her had caused the confusing effect.

"What are you doing here?" Dave asked her. The confusion was plain in his voice.

"I came here to talk with you."

"Why here? Couldn't we just talk at home?"

Debbie just smiled and shook her head. "I love you, Dave."

"I love you too, honey. Why did you come here to tell me that though?"

"You know, sweetie. I want you to wake up."

"But it's the middle of the night," he told her. As soon as he said the words it was instantly night. The stars dotted the sky and a sliver of moon peeked out from behind a cloud.

Debbie shook her lovely head again. "Dave, you need to wake up and get back to living."

"What do you mean?" He asked her, becoming very confused. "We had our problems, but we are doing better now. I'm really trying. You know that, right?"

"I know, baby," she told him as she stepped up to him and put her hand on the side of his face.

Dave could smell her perfume as he breathed her in.

"You need to wake up now," she told him again.

Dave looked around and realized he was all alone. An overwhelming sense of loss crashed down on him, tears fell freely from his eyes.

Chapter 30

The sunlight was streaming in through the eastern facing windows. Mornings like these seemed to be what he really enjoyed. He would turn his face to the sun and even occasionally smile as the sun warmed his skin. She liked to see him smile. It sure beat his silent tears. When Dave smiled the years seamed to melt right off of him. She thought she could imagine the man he had been, that he was a man that laughed a lot, and who had been warm and caring.

She liked to imagine him that way anyway. She knew a little about his history: that he was a husband and father, and a businessman who had provided well for his family. She knew that his father had not been in his life and his mother only stopped by to visit him once in all the time he'd been here. His mom had sat in the room with her son for only a half an hour and had then left without any expression on her face. With parents like that she knew that her imaginings that Dave had been a man that laughed a lot was her fantasy and likely had not been reality. Even so, it was nice to imagine him that way. It helped her feel closer to him.

Dave was one of the easiest to care for, but also the most unresponsive. The doctors said that there wasn't anything more they could do for him.

He had days when he was actually "here," but those days were very few and far between, and, in her opinion, they were the worst for him. From the time he realized where he was until he faded away, he was either crying from what seemed to be the depths of his soul, yelling until his voice gave out that it was all his fault, seemingly babbling to himself as he shook his head from side to side, or simply staring off into nothingness.

It seemed to her that Dave didn't want to be in the "here and now." He wanted to be left to his dreams. The days when he was lucid were the worst for him. At least when he was away, as she called it, he seemed to be happy.

Most of the time he just sat still, and she would wipe the drool from his chin and make sure he was okay. She didn't know what he was dreaming about, but it was better than what he realized his reality was, when he was awake.

She couldn't blame him. Maybe it was better if he stayed dreaming, instead of dealing with the pain of reality.

She continued to talk with him. She told him what was going on in the news, about her latest boyfriend or lack there-of. She complained about how hard it was to find a good man, even though it seemed as if all her friends knew a prince charming that she simply had to go out with.

"Dave," she said, "I wish more men would simply listen to what a woman has to say like you do." Although she said it partly as a joke, she really did mean it. It seemed that all men today wanted to do was to talk about their success or their insecurities. "Whoever told men that they needed to express their sensitive side did not make it clear to some men. They seemed to think that it meant they had to 'convince' you they were sensitive in this day and age. Well baby, I am not the kind of woman that needs convincing. I need a man to show me what he is about." She paused and looked at him for a minute before shaking her head.

"Honey, you've listened to me go on for long enough. Here I am, yet again, going on and on about my problems. I haven't even let you get in a word edgewise."

"What's that Dave? … I know, sugar! Everything will be alright in the end. Wiser words have never been spoken."

"I see you're lost in thought again. I'll tell you what, while you ponder the universe or whatever it is that has you so entranced, I'll leave you to it and see you tomorrow like always. Have a good night honey." She walked out of the door gently closing it behind her.

Chapter 31

"So, what did the doctor tell you?" Aidan asked Julie.

"He said that the lining of my stomach is inflamed," she responded.

"Okay, but that is the symptom of the problem. Did he tell you what he thinks is causing it?" he asked her.

"Relax honey, he said it's probably nothing to worry about. He said lots of girls my age go through this. He told me that it is normal for it to be the worst in the morning and then get better as the day goes on. Maybe it's just nerves. Finals are coming up, and I know that I haven't been studying as much as I should be," She told him.

"Julie you and I both know that's not it. You've been studying as much as you always do."

"Not true," she responded. "I happen to be spending a lot of my dear study time with a handsome boy that has swept me off of my feet. I am simply helpless to stop myself from spending time with him. No matter how hard I try, I have to tell him yes, when he asks me out. The sad thing is the lout knows how much time I need to concentrate to get good grades."

"Oh really," Aidan replied. "You just tell me who this guy is, and I will rip his head off. Nobody messes with my girl."

"Seriously, honey, are you worried about the exams?" Aidan asked her.

"Well, I didn't think that I was, but maybe I am stressing more than I should be." She paused. She was so tempted to tell him. He had a right to know she thought. Her mother had told her that the best thing to do was to wait until the first trimester had passed. She had told her that most pregnancies *"didn't take"* as she said it. As it turned out Google agreed with her. Her long pause was still hanging in the air between them. "You know what, forget it. I'm sure that I'm worried about nothing. Come here and give me a kiss. Make me forget about all of these problems.

As much as Aidan wanted to shower her with kisses, he paused, "Are you sure that everything is okay? You know you can tell me anything, right?"

That was one thing about Aidan. He was good at catching the details.

Julie was scared to bring up a discussion about pregnancy. She didn't want to scare him away. Like her mom said, most often the pregnancy didn't take. Why tell him if it turned out to be nothing? What were the odds anyway?

She laughed and told him: “Relax the bug is probably passing even as we speak.”

With that, they started to talk about what they were going to do on Saturday night. There was a really good movie Julie had heard about. It was a romance, but it was supposed to have good action in it too. It sounded like something they both would enjoy. She told him about the movie and was surprised to hear that he had also been looking forward to watching it. With that settled they decided to go out for dinner and then the movie. There was a really good seafood place that Julie’s mom and dad had gone to on one of their “Us Time” nights as they referred to them. They told Julie about the place and even recommended that Julie and Aidan should try the halibut. Her dad said it was the best he had ever had.

Chapter 32

Dave was bored. *How was that even possible*? Since getting the satellite installed for the TV, he had discovered that having more channels did not mean that there was more that he wanted to see. In fact, on nights like this, when both Aidan and Summer were out with their friends, and Debbie was sleeping before working the late shift, he found that there were more shows that he didn't want to see than ones he was interested in. On top of that, he had discovered the "shopping channels." In his opinion, these were the worst of all. Why would anyone shop like this? It was so much better to go into a store, and actually see the product, then, if there were any questions, simply ask the salesperson. It seemed so impersonal to call in and buy a product over the phone. Then again, there must be some people who were shopping this way. If not, then there wouldn't be so many channels dedicated to it. *Oh well*, he thought, *it's not like I need to understand it. I don't understand how anyone can watch these daytime soap operas either and look how long they have been on TV. I guess there is no accounting for taste.*

"Hey, Dad!" Summer called, as she came into the living room. "Whatcha watchin'?"

"I'm watchin' a whole lot of nothing, to be honest," he told her. "I can't believe that we have so many channels and there is nothing worth watching."

"Well Dad, you know what they say?" she asked him. "Two hundred and forty-seven channels and nothing on!"

In reality, he wanted to be doing something and was very happy that Summer was home. He hoped she was not planning on going out again. He really wanted to spend some time with her. Lately, she had been so busy that they were not able to spend time together like he wanted.

"Honey are you going to be home for the rest of the night?" he asked her.

She had planned on going over to Tammy's house later, to study with her, but one look at her Dad's face as he asked her made up her mind for her.

"No Dad, I'm going to stay in tonight," she told him and saw his face break into a big smile.

"That's great news!" he exclaimed. "I think that if I spent the whole night glued to the TV, I would probably lose my mind." He made a completely blank face with his tongue sticking out of the corner of his mouth.

"You are such a goof!" Summer stated as she broke out laughing.

"Hey, what do you say we do something nice for mom?" he asked her. "You know she has the late-shift tonight at the hospital?"

Summer nodded her head.

"Well, I was thinking that we could have dinner ready for her when she woke up. I was thinking we could have taco night." Dave declared. "Does that sound good to you?"

"Yes, I can't wait. You know I love taco night."

"Okay, honey. Let me just take a look and see if we have everything we need?" He opened up the refrigerator door and looked inside. "We have hamburger but it looks like we will need lettuce and tomatoes. Summer can you look in the pantry to see if we have taco shells still?"

"Well, we do, but I don't think that we should use them," she answered him.

"Why not?" he asked her.

"Well, if you don't mind eating them, even though they are over six months past their expiration date, then okay. Me, though, I think I would prefer some fresh ones!" she said with a disapproving look on her face.

Dave laughed at how serious she was about the expiration date. "Okay, taco shells too," he agreed.

"We'll pop on over to the grocery store and pick these things up. Let me take a quick look around and see what else we need while we are there," said Dave.

With list in hand, they went to gather the groceries.

Once they were home again, they fell into a routine. Summer had always been good around the kitchen, she often helped Debbie with cooking. Debbie had started teaching her how to cook when she was only four years old. That was when Debbie had appointed her as official pancake batter stirrer. She even got to use the official stirring fork! Summer enjoyed helping out, and soon was asking questions about how to know when to flip the pancakes. What makes the cake get bigger in the oven? Why does the water get bubbles in it when it gets hot? And about a million other questions that add up to an education in the kitchen.

Father and daughter worked well as a team and were just about finished when they heard Debbie come into the kitchen asking, “What is all this for?”

“We just thought you would like a good meal before you went to work,” answered Summer.

“That was very sweet of you, honey,” said Debbie as she wrapped her daughter in her arms and gave her a kiss on her forehead.

“Hey, I helped out some too,” said Dave. “Can I get in on some of that too?”

“Come on over here,” Debbie said, as she put her arms around both of them and held on tight.

They stayed like that for a little while, hugging each other in the middle of the kitchen.

“Come on now,” said Debbie. “If we don’t hurry, we will be eating cold tacos!”

When they were finishing up eating, Debbie looked at the clock and said, “Sorry to be a party pooper, but I have to get to work. I really wish I was off tonight. It would be great to just sit down and watch a movie together.”

“Mom, that does sound good. Will you have next weekend off?” asked Summer.

“Yeah, I do. That sounds like a plan!” said Debbie.

“You didn’t even have time to eat any of the ice cream,” Dave reminded her.

“I’ll have some for breakfast when I come home. Save some for me okay?” she asked.

“Well, I don’t usually have cream with my coffee, but for a woman as beautiful as you I will make an exception,” teased Dave before he gave her a long kiss.

“You two can be really gross sometimes, you know?” said Summer.

Dave and Debbie looked at each other smiling and answered, “Yeah we know it!”

Debbie went off to her shift at the hospital and Summer and Dave settled in the family room to watch a comedy. All in all, it was a good night.

Chapter 33

Dave reached out and picked up the ringing phone.

"Hello?" he mumbled.

He cracked open his eyes enough to see what time it was; 12:17AM. That brought him instantly alert as he registered Debbie talking to him on the other end of the line.

"Dave! Wake up!" Debbie screamed at him over the line.

"What happened?"

"Dave, get Summer up and come to the hospital!" said Debbie in her get things done now tone. "Aidan was in an accident. Get here as quick as you can!"

"We'll be right there, honey." Dave realized he was talking to a dead phone; Debbie had already hung up.

One thought kept running through his mind. "This couldn't be happening. Not Aidan!"

"Summer get up honey," he called out.

"What is it, Dad?"

"Aidan's been in an accident. We need to get to the hospital."

They were out the door in less than five minutes. Dave fought the urge to race down the nearly deserted streets. He knew that getting into an accident or being stopped by the police would only delay them further.

Debbie was waiting for them at the entrance to the ER. She was barely keeping herself under control.

"Come on, follow me."

"How bad is it, honey?" he asked her.

She just shook her head and kept walking towards the back of the ER. Before she reached the doors to the surgery area her legs buckled. Dave barely caught her from falling. Debbie twisted her torso in his arms and buried her face in her husband's chest and started to cry.

He looked up at Summer. She looked lost. She didn't know what to do. She kept looking down at her mother and then back to the door they'd been walking towards. Her eyes kept focusing on the word Surgery.

Debbie finally got herself enough under control to say: "They won't let me go in Dave." She buried her head in his shoulder as she choked out, "I don't think he's going to make it. He's in really bad shape."

He held her to him as he sat down and leaned up against the wall. Out of the corner of his eye, he saw Summer lean back against the wall for support.

Dave had no way of knowing how much time passed. It seemed like he waited for an eternity in that quiet, stringently clean, brightly lit hallway. At the same time, everything was a blur, so the minutes blurred together. He had lost all perspective.

Sometime later, people began filing out of the operating room. Some of them looked over at them and then quickly turned their eyes away. Dave feared the worst, but he still held out hope, until a tall man knelt down with them and slowly shook his head.

"I am so sorry Debbie. We couldn't save him."

"Dead? He can't be dead. He's too young to be dead. My son can't be dead!" Dave realized he was talking out loud. He also realized that he was holding Debbie up. Summer had slid down the wall and was sitting on the floor, hugging her knees.

A couple of nurses arrived to guide them from the hall outside of the room where Aidan's lifeless body now lay. Nothing was making any sense. This couldn't be happening, and yet, he knew that it was. They were guided to a quiet room and left to their grief. When she was able to, Debbie told them, what had happened.

"Aidan and Julie went to watch a movie over at the new Cineplex, the one in Greenville. They were on their way home when it started to rain. They came upon a woman trying to change the tire on her car in the downpour. Aidan, of course, pulled over to help her. Julie told me that he looked at her and said, 'you know we should, right?' and they agreed.

"Julie waited in the truck while Aidan helped the woman. It was Mrs. Johnston, the third-grade teacher, and her two kids." Debbie wiped her nose with a soggy tissue.

"She's in surgery right now, Mrs. Johnston that is. The kids are okay though," Debbie looked at Dave's puzzled expression. "Sorry, the kids were in the car, out of the rain. They had some minor cuts and will be sore for a couple of days, but they are okay."

"Aidan was almost done with the tire when he was hit by a truck. A guy, I don't know who he is, was coming back from Smitty's Bar and Grill, drunk as a skunk. His girlfriend left him today, so he was drowning his sorrows. The police took him away earlier. He didn't even get a scratch on him. Can you believe that? The police officer, Bill Jennings, assured me that a full investigation would be done, and he would keep us up to date."

"Dave, Aidan pushed Mrs. Johnston out of the way when he saw the truck coming at them. She'd been holding an umbrella, trying to keep Aidan dry." Dave saw the look of pride at Aidan's bravery and selflessness on her face. "Turns out it was enough to save her life. The truck hit her legs when it smashed into her car, but if Aidan hadn't pushed her, she would have been crushed in between the two vehicles. Aidan tried to jump out of the way, Julie told me. There just wasn't time." She said with her voice trailing off to little more than a whisper.

"Julie's over in trauma four with her parents. The truck hit Aidan's truck before it hit the Johnston woman's car. Julie has a cut on her cheek and possible whiplash to her neck. She said that the impact made her head hit the window pretty hard. She didn't black out but said she wished she had, that way she wouldn't have seen the fear on Aidan's face."

"Julie will be fine, other than a small cut and a bump on her head and some mild shock. She's okay. Oh . . . There is one other thing." A small smile pushed up the corners of her mouth. She reached out and took Dave and Summer's hand into her own. "She's pregnant. About three months along, so it looks like we're going to be grandparents." With that Debbie broke down into wracking sobs.

This recounting of the events did not come in such a straightforward manner. It came out over the course of several hours, broken up by fits of crying and long periods of silence.

Dave sat there stunned, holding his wife. Summer was on her knees in front of her mom. She was hugging her and resting her head on Debbie's lap. They stayed like that for quite a while. Time had lost relevance; it was still moving on, but on another level, it had stopped. Aidan's time had come to an end.

Dave held on to Debbie and Summer, but all the while his soul was calling out for his son.

No response was to be heard from Aidan. The deafening silence echoed in the void of the broken hearts left behind.

Dave opened his eyes to a room that had people sitting around tables. These people were different somehow. They were there but did not seem to be *all* there somehow. He had a feeling that he knew this place. Yes, he knew this place, and he knew it well. It was a place where he didn't want to be. A warm fire was burning in the fireplace in the center of the room. More of the people that were there but yet were not fully there were gathered around the fireplace. He knew what that meant, but it was not important right then.

He felt the loss of Aidan tearing him apart. The pain was unbearable! He raised his face to the ceiling and what started out as a whisper from his un-used vocal cords rapidly rose to a bellow of rage. "NOOOOOOoooooooooooooooooo!" He raged at everything, at the loss of Aidan.

Chantal ran over to stop Dave. He was banging his fist on the table and shouting at the top of his lungs. He kept shouting NO! Over and over again. He was getting louder every time he hit the table. As she reached him, she heard him better.

"No! It can't be! No! They can't be dead! NO!" *Slam*! "NO!" *Slam*! "No! It can't be! NO! They can't be dead!" Over and over again.

"Dave!" Chantal said next to his ear.

"No! It can't be!" Dave went on as if she wasn't there.

He was lost inside his own hell.

"Calm down, sugar," Chantal said to him in her soothing voice as she caressed his face. She hoped to distract him from the rage that had gripped him. She had never seen him this upset over anything! He had never demonstrated such emotion. Sure, he had cried his heart out and occasionally had yelled, but nothing like this.

He was really working himself up.

Chantal was rapidly becoming concerned about his blood pressure. Dave's face was going from red to a shade of purple that did not look good. He wasn't getting enough oxygen. His breaths were coming in little gasps.

Chantal kept talking with him in her most soothing voice. "It will be okay," she kept telling him over and over again.

Dave slumped over and simply folded in on himself. He was exhausted both physically and emotionally. He stayed that way for a long time, slumped in his wheelchair.

Chantal moved him, so he could sit in front of the fireplace. The warmth and the crackling of the burning wood helped to keep him relaxed. She stayed with him past the end of her shift. She sat in a chair next to him, holding his hand and talking with him in her reassuring voice. In time, he drifted off to a calming, healing sleep. She sat there for a while longer idly rubbing her thumb on the back of his hand.

Chapter 34

Time resolutely moved on, as it always does, and things eventually fell into a new rhythm. They cried, they got into little stupid arguments over nothing, they would find each other staring at nothing at all for long periods of time. Other times, they would just let each other be. Sometimes, one or the other would give a hug.

Dave found it amazing how good a hug could feel at times like that; that need to hold onto each other was what, in the end, kept them from completely falling apart. Often, he thought he was losing his grip on things and he didn't know how he made it from one moment to the next, let alone to another day.

Another day without Aidan in it.

"What a damn shame!" Dave raged yet again. "It's not fair. I mean I know that it is never fair. No death at that age is ever fair. It's just not right to have your child die, leaving you alive to deal with the pain."

Time moved on and eventually so did they. It didn't happen overnight, of course, but Aidan would not have wanted them to quit living. He had always been so full of life. Dave tried to honor his memory by looking for ways to appreciate the days he had.

Every single day he talked with him. He set aside time to tell him about things that he thought he would be interested in. He shared with him things that were happening in the news, the little things that were going on in the family. And he made it a rule to always tell Aidan the truth, which included telling him his honest feelings about things. Dave didn't know if Aidan was able to see them from wherever he was now, but he liked to think that he could. It really helped him to deal with his loss.

He missed him so much. He never knew there could be pain like this.

Summer dealt with the loss of her brother in her own way. Dave was concerned with the direction her grieving had taken her. He was worried that she would derail a bright future by shutting down emotionally. Dave and Debbie had talked about it and had decided that it was normal, whatever normal could be in a situation like this, that she closed herself off a little. They didn't think there was a problem when she didn't go back to hanging out with her friends. She would just come home and then go to her room and close the door. If they knocked on her door, she always said "come in" right away. They tried to not dwell on the fact that she wasn't talking with her friends, that she wasn't talking with them much either. Then again, maybe they were a little too distracted with how they felt to pay enough attention to her.

Debbie was having trouble finding her balance if that was the right thing to say when you lose someone as essential to your existence as your son. Hell, what was the right thing to say when your son was taken away from you by such a preventable accident? That made it even harder to bear.

Dave's mind always returned to pondering three essential questions, the 'what if' questions that all came to the same answer. Aidan would still be alive:

What if - that damn drunk had leaned in his seat left instead of right.

What if - he had run himself into a ditch before coming across our Aidan.

Hell, if he had simply gone home with a bottle and drank himself stupid in the safety of his own home our son would still be with us."

"So many what-ifs and none of them do anyone a damn bit of good!"

Aidan was gone.

Julie was going to be a single mom, and their child was not going to know his father. The only connection he would have with him would be through stories and pictures. What an empty shell compared to what Aidan would have given him.

What a tragedy!

Aidan would have been a great dad. He was so patient and smart. He was also funny.

The sound of the sigh that escaped from Dave's lips gave sound to how spent he felt inside. Thinking this for the millionth time. He reached up and absently wiped a tear from his cheek He reminded himself that, in the end, life goes on either with or without us.

He raised his eyes to the ceiling until the urge to cry passed. It never went away, it simply dwindled for a while. It would return at the strangest times. He would find himself suddenly just getting choked up. Most of the time he could hold it off until he was in private, but sometimes, it came on so strong that he couldn't fight it off.

The loss of Aidan was hard on everyone, but it had been especially hard on Debbie. Dave was really beginning to worry that she simply didn't care to keep going on. It was as if she had simply given up on life. She was staying in bed most of the day.

Before that night, she couldn't stay in bed after she woke up, she was one of those people that had to get up and get going. Now, more-often-than-not, she told him that she simply was too tired. She was too tired to not only get out of bed but, even when she did get out of bed, she only lay down on the couch, staring with vacant eyes at the television. When she said she was tired Dave believed her. She looked exhausted.

When he looked at his beautiful wife all he saw was a shadow of what she had been before that fateful night. Her eyes were sunken and had dark rings under them, her complexion had turned waxy. Now he understood what a 'waxy complexion' looked like. He wished to God he didn't. She had obviously lost weight too. Her clothes hung off her emaciated frame and Dave observed her skin hanging loosely from her arms. She told him that she had no appetite when he urged her to eat more. She wasn't interested in eating or, to be honest, doing anything at all anymore. Well, except looking through old photo albums.

One afternoon Dave decided that they needed to talk about what was going on. As usual, she was sitting on the couch, the TV was on and she was looking through one of the photo albums. Dave sat down next to her and looked at the pictures of their son with her.

After a little while he decided it was time to talk about what he came here to say. "Debbie, I'm worried about you," he said to her as he rubbed her back. "I'm worried that you don't want to do anything anymore. I know it's hard. There are days that I don't want to face the world either. I make myself do it though. Life goes on." He touched the side of her face and turned it to face him. "We have to go on. Summer needs us, baby. We have to help her. We have to be there for her."

"I know. I know you are right." She started crying and was not able to talk for a little bit. Dave put his arm around her and held her close.

"I feel so empty. I don't have anything left to give to her. I have nothing left," said Debbie in a voice barely more than a whisper.

"You do, sweetie. You have so much love in you. Your pain is just covering everything up now. That pain is not going away. I don't think it should either. We have to push through it though and let our love for Summer come through too. She needs us. Even if we don't have much to give her now, we have to try. We have to be there for her."

"Dave, I just can't. I don't think I have anything left to give to her. I feel like all that is left is an empty shell."

He had an inspiration. "What do you think if your mom came here for a while? She's been offering to help out. I think it would really be a good thing."

Debbie looked at him and nodded her head. She then hugged him tightly to her and cried. The idea of her mom being there gave her a feeling of relief. Maybe she could get through this.

When she got herself under control, she sat up again.

"Do you want to call her now," Dave asked her.

"No, there's something I need to do first."

Debbie went up to Summer's room and lightly tapped on her door.

"Come in."

Summer was sitting up on her bed reading a book.

Debbie sat down next to her and held out her arms. Summer could see the tear tracks on her mother's cheeks. She put her book down and went into her mother's embrace.

"I'm sorry I haven't been here for you more." Debbie let her tears flow.

Summer didn't try to hold back her tears, she didn't try to say anything, she just held onto her mother and felt safe in her arms.

Chapter 35

Gail arrived the next day with two suitcases in tow. She obviously planned to stay as long as needed. Things didn't get better all at once. Debbie knew that she needed to snap out of this funk that had settled over her, but knowing it, and having the energy to do something about it was something else altogether. They could see the defeat that clung on her as clear as day.

Debbie's mother opened up the curtains around the house and let some light and air come into what had begun to feel like a mausoleum. She even turned on the radio, and with music in the air, went to work straightening up the house. They had really allowed it to become a mess.

Debbie had lost interest in keeping it as tidy as she had before. It had always been her that went behind all of them and cleaned up, fussing at them if they left things out of their place. She didn't complain about it, she just reminded them that they all had a part to play in keeping their home tidy. But, lately, nobody had been doing their part. That came to an end today. It was time to get things slowly back on track.

Things would never be the same without Aidan, but they had a life to live. It was time that they started living it again.

A few days later Debbie and her mother were sitting in the back-yard sipping their coffee. A light breeze was blowing through the trees. The air was cool. The temperature would be dropping soon with fall coming on. The sun that was filtering its way through the leaves was enough to keep them warm. The sound of the birds singing was nice.

They'd been talking about the work her mom was doing in her backyard. She had a green thumb and was always planting something new. After a while she thought that she had talked enough about her gardening and went into what she really wanted to talk about.

She reached across the table and held Debbie's hand. She didn't say anything at first. They just sat there holding hands.

"What can I do to help, honey?"

"Mom, just having you here is wonderful. I have been feeling so alone and empty."

Gail knew better than to say anything. She gave her hand a reassuring squeeze and waited for her to continue.

"Dave has been very understanding. I know you and dad were just a call away, but I didn't want to bother you," she said with her eyes focused on her cup of coffee. "I know Mom, it would be no bother so don't say it. I didn't want to bother you though. Do you understand?" Debbie looked at her mom and saw that she did.

"I didn't want to reach out to anyone. I hurt *so* much, Mom."

"Honey, do you need to talk with someone? Maybe some grief counseling?"

"I don't know. I don't know if talking about it will make it better. Better!" She spat out the word. "There is no 'better'! He's gone, Mom."

They sat out there for most of the afternoon. They talked. They cried. They even laughed a little.

When they came back inside Debbie made a phone call and set up an appointment for grief counseling.

The counselor came over to the house and had a long talk with her. Dave and Gail left them alone to start working on the depression that had settled so strongly on her.

Dave found it hard to believe that the strong energetic woman he had known for the better part of his life had been reduced to the shell she now was. It was almost as if he had lost two people that night.

Dave went out for a little while. When he came back home the counselor had gone and Debbie was sitting at the kitchen table with her mom. They were both drinking coffees.

Dave poured himself a cup and joined them.

"I'm going to keep meeting with her. I feel comfortable talking with her. Maybe it'll do some good."

"Honey, that's a great idea," said Dave.

She cut him off by raising a finger.

"Dave, I want you to know that I know I need the treatment. I know I'm in a state of depression. We talked about that and I was able to distance myself enough to realize the clinical symptoms. I know I'm not handling this very well." A look of such pain twisted her face. With an effort she forced her face to relax and got her breathing back to normal. "I know that Summer needs more than I have been able to give her." Her eyes locked onto his. "I love her." She lowered her eyes back to her cup of coffee. "I also realize that we need to get counseling as a family. We need to work on our family communication. It will be good for all of us."

"Here's the card she gave me. I'm going to do this for our daughter. She deserves better than I have given her. We need to help her to get back into her life. Dave, do you remember how good of a kid she is? She really is a good person. She deserves more of what she had. I mean when we were a family."

"Do you remember what it was like when we lived on Elm Street? Do you remember how we used to like playing with the kids and laughing? I can't even remember the last time I laughed like that. With simple joy. Do you remember what that was like, Dave?"

"No, I guess I don't."

"Well, we owe it to Summer to let her find her way back to that. I owe it to her! I'm going to try as hard as I can."

Chapter 36

Spring was blooming, and the trees were covered in buds. The birds were returning and bringing their beautiful voices with them. Dave was sitting in the back yard drinking his first cup of coffee. The air was still a bit brisk, but it was a good way to wake up. He had a lot on his mind lately. Debbie was doing better, but things had been distant between them. He understood that she did not feel comfortable with intimacy. He kept telling himself to give it time.

But I have given it time. There comes a point when I will have to admit that this is the way it is. Okay, so I am not trying as much as I used to. I have to be honest with myself, at least when I am holding an active conversation with myself.

In fact, he had been doing worse than not trying, he'd been actively avoiding Debbie. There are only so many times that a man can be rejected before he stops trying. Well, at least there was for him. It wasn't just about being rejected for sex. He was sure that other men would have already left her, for that alone, but he was not one of those men. Other men would have gone out and cheated. It wasn't that long ago that he thought that men who did things like that were all hormonally crazed and couldn't or wouldn't control themselves. Lately, he had developed a new perspective on things, and his opinion had evolved. Sure, there were, and would always be, those that cheat to satisfy their own urges, either physical or out of a sense of control. He had recently come to realize that there likely was another group, a group that wasn't ready to completely give up on what they had, but still had a substantial need for companionship. A need to have someone that wanted them to touch them, to hold them, to *be with them*. For Dave it was that last part that had him thinking more and more about becoming one of *those* guys.

The last time he had made an effort, to be intimate, was still very fresh in his mind. He thought back to that day. It had been a rough day at the office. Well, to be honest, he realized that it was his fault as well. He remembered that he went to the office already in a bad mood. No matter what happened he was grumpy, and the smallest thing set him off. By the time he got home he was wound up pretty tight. All he wanted to do was relax with a glass of wine, or three. He was giving off some pretty clear signs because Summer finished her dinner quickly and then went up to her room.

Debbie was in the living room watching TV. He didn't want another fight, so he sat at the table for a while after he had finished eating. All he wanted was to just put the day behind him. He finished his glass of wine and felt like he had himself pretty firmly under control, so he decided to join Debbie in the living room.

"What's on?" he asked her.

"Nothing, same as usual," was her response as she clicked through channel after channel. After about a half hour of this she threw down the remote in disgust and slunk out of the room.

He sat there for a couple of hours more. He didn't remember what he had watched. He kept thinking that he wanted things to be better, he wanted them to be like they used to be. He wanted that attraction, that desire, that longing, the companionship. He wanted to finish work and look forward to coming home, not dread walking in the door just knowing that there was either going to be a fight over something that was not really important or, even worse, a night of silence.

He reasoned, someone has to make the effort or things will only get worse. That nagging voice in his head reminded him with each step, and quite a few reminders in-between steps, just how many times he had tried to bring them closer together. *Tried and failed*, his nagging voice clarified, as if he needed the reminder.

He had put away all of his self-doubts and climbed into their bed. He couldn't tell if Debbie was awake or sleeping. If she was sleeping, he didn't want to wake her. He knew how little she'd been sleeping lately. If she was awake, he didn't want to disturb her either. He only wanted to be close to her, to hold her in his arms. He wanted to feel like they were together again, if only for a little while.

He snuggled up to her back and put his arm on her shoulder. After a couple minutes, he moved his hand to her stomach.

"I just want to sleep, don't be mad." Debbie rolled away.

He rolled onto his back and tried to sort through his confused emotions. He wasn't mad. He was hurt. He understood what was going on, but that didn't make it any easier to deal with. No matter how you looked at it, Dave needed affection and Debbie wasn't giving it to him. She was rejecting him. He tried to be understanding, but it was getting harder to do.

Dave decided that enough time had gone by. He resolved that he was going to start working on his marriage again. Finished with his coffee, he went in to the kitchen and looked at Debbie's work schedule on the side of the fridge. She had Wednesday off this week. That meant that date night was going to be Tuesday. She would be coming off a late shift Tuesday morning and would have plenty of time to sleep before he wined and dined her.

Chapter 37

Summer hadn't been dealing with the loss of her brother well at all either. The difference was, that she kept up a good act at home, so she didn't worry her parents any more than they already were. Her parents were so self-absorbed, trying to deal with Aidan's loss, in their own way. They just hurt too much, to hurt each other anymore, by telling how much pain they were really in.

Summer was a good girl. She studied hard, and had good friends, she didn't stay out late and was pretty even tempered. She didn't have the temper tantrums or teenage angst that you heard about all the time. But, since the accident, her grades had slipped. Her last report card showed that she had dropped two letter grades in three of the seven classes she was taking. She was even failing one class.

When Dave asked her about it, he had made it a point to have a discussion, and not come down on her about it. She was going through a lot, and if she slipped off the grade curve for one semester, that was very understandable.

Well, the talk went pretty much as expected. Since the accident she'd lost interest in a lot of things and had drifted without a sense of direction for a while. She told him that the report card had been an eye opener for her as well. She said that she had already started to study harder and was working on bringing her grades back up. In fact, she said that she had already talked with Mr. Greenburgh about doing some extra credit for the Geography class that she was currently failing.

Dave was encouraged that she had taken the initiative of talking with her teacher on her own. It looked to him, that she was starting to come around, and take control of her life again. To say he was relieved would be an understatement. It felt really uplifting to have something good happen again.

There was a knock at the door. Summer turned down her music and listened to see if she had really heard a knock or if it had been her imagination. After a couple of seconds, she heard the doorbell chime.

Summer went down the stairs and was surprised to see who was standing there.

“Julie!” exclaimed Summer. “This is a wonderful surprise! Come in.” Summer stepped back to make room for Julie to get by with her very pregnant belly.

“How much longer?” asked Summer looking at Julie’s belly.

“Three more weeks.”

“Julie, you look beautiful,” Summer said.

“Oh, stop it! I look like a whale and you know it,” Julie replied.

“You do not! I have heard that pregnant girls have a glow about them. I never believed it, but you are really glowing!”

"I don't know about all of that, but I'll tell you one thing that it might be from, I'm eating all of the right kinds of food. I have never eaten so many vegetables in all of my life." She groaned, making a funny face. "Seriously though, I feel really good. Well, except for needing to go pee every five minutes."

"How have you been doing, apart from the pregnancy?" Summer asked. "I can't even remember the last time we sat down and talked."

"It has been a long time," Julie agreed. They talked about little things, small talk. Caught up on their mutual friends. Summer filled her in on how the soccer season went. "Enough about me," said Summer. "How've you been?"

Julie took a deep breath. "Well, at first things were pretty bad. I didn't know what to do. I really wanted to just die. I'm not proud of that, but I did. I just wanted the pain to stop. I wanted everything to stop. I hurt *so* much. I love Aidan so much and all-of-a-sudden, he was just gone. It isn't right. He should be with me. I should be able to hear his laugh. Do you remember his laugh?"

"Yeah, I do. He laughed like he meant it. That's the best way for me to describe it. When he laughed it was sincere and you could tell that he really felt it. Aidan was never fake," Summer said.

"Yeah, that was it. He felt it. He really felt it and you could tell that he did. I miss him so much," Julie said, and she broke down. Both gave in to their emotions as they shared their feelings. Summer held Julie close and they both let the pain of losing Aidan out. They just let it go. It felt good to talk about missing Aidan with someone that really understood what that meant.

They told each other what they had been through, and it felt really good to be talking about the hardships they had been forced to endure. Summer told her about the way she had been cast out of her normal circle of friends. She even told her about her relationship with Tammy. Summer found it strange to be telling anyone about Tammy. Her relationship with Tammy had somehow become a secret. That, in part, was the problem. There was nothing wrong with her being friends with Tammy. She should not feel ashamed of having a good friend like her.

Julie was understanding of the things that she had been through. Since there were only a few years difference in age, things at school hadn't changed much. Instead of leaving for college, Julie had decided to stay close to home. She'd been taking classes at the community college to satisfy her lower level classes. She would see about her college education one step at a time. For now, she couldn't manage more than a class or two at a time. Once the baby was born, she knew she was going to have her hands full. One step at a time.

Summer felt a closeness with Julie that she didn't feel with anyone else. She imagined that if she had an older sister, she would feel like this toward her. That was when she realized that, in a very real sense, Julie was like an older sister to her. Inside her, grew the child of her lost brother. That was a bond like no other.

They talked through the afternoon before Summer suggested Julie stay for dinner. Julie readily accepted this invitation.

Things had been different between Julie and her mom since the accident. Things were very strained. Her mother had been understanding of her loss and gave her the room to grieve Aidan. The tension came over the baby. Her mom and dad were a united front and they believed she should have an abortion. Of course, they didn't come right out and say that at first. Julie always knew they would though. She expected their stance back when she thought she was late with her period. Now that the confrontation was over Julie knew she had made the right decision.

She understood how hard it was going to be to raise a baby on her own, but it was Aidan's child. There was no way she could abort all that she had left of Aidan. She had seriously considered adoption as an option. Her child deserved the best out of life and she was practical enough to realize the challenges she was going to face.

Her parents were on her all the time to do "something" about her "condition". Sometimes her mother made it sound as if she had caught a cold instead of getting pregnant. There were some pretty bad fights and things were said between Julie and her mother that changed their relationship forever.

It was her father that had changed the most. He'd always been an understanding man and after the accident he'd been the one that had urged her mom to give her more time to get over the accident. The big change in him happened during the heated discussions over abortion. He was convinced that the best thing to do was to put the whole thing behind her and move on with her life.

When Julie strongly rejected getting an abortion he withdrew. Julie wondered if, in time, he'd be able to forgive her for not honoring his wishes. In this though, she simply couldn't do it. She couldn't end the life of Aidan's child and that was that.

Julie had kept her distance from Aidan's family until she had known what she was going to do about the baby. She didn't want to add their feelings to her already difficult decision.

Now that she was secure in her decision, she had decided to try to mend her relationship with Aidan's family. The life that was growing in her, made her one of the family. She had been pretty close to Aidan's parents. She knew they were good people and hoped that she'd be welcomed into the family. She was determined to do so.

The dinner went well. They caught up on what had happened in their lives. They kept the focus on Julie and the life growing inside her.

Chapter 38

Debbie was slowly coming back. The sessions with her counselor seemed to be working for her. It didn't happen overnight, but she was taking small steps, back to where she had been. After some time, and changes in medication, she was getting back to doing some of the things she did before that fateful night. She had taken a couple of weeks off from work at the beginning, anticipating a difficult time. She ended up needing to go on an extended medical leave.

She had tried to go back to work at the end of the two weeks. Half-way through the first day one of her friends, Susan, drove her back home, calling Dave from the house when they got there. Susan had been a friend of Debbie's for years.

Dave had been dreading a call all day. He knew the magnitude of Debbie going back to work so soon and feared the worst.

Susan, to her credit, jumped right to the heart of the matter. "Debbie had a rough first day back. We're back at your house. She's okay, Dave."

"Thank you, Susan, I'll be right there."

"No Dave, relax, everything is under control. I have a bottle of wine open and we are going to talk the afternoon away, or maybe we're going to cry the afternoon away. Either way, it will be okay. I can't even imagine the pain you are both going through. I am here for her. It's okay."

When Dave came home, Debbie had already gone up to lie down and Susan was busy straightening up the house. He quickly thanked her for being there for Debbie. She insisted on staying until she was done. He assured her that appreciated her help and he wanted her to come around and check on how Debbie was doing. He kept telling her how very grateful he was for her being there for Debbie. She was truly a good friend. The whole time all he wanted to do was to have her leave, so he could go to his wife.

He was so frustrated with her condition. He wanted to fix her. He wanted to make it all better and he couldn't do it. He couldn't make this all better, but he could be there for her. He could be there to hold her.

Debbie had not anticipated being completely knocked out of herself. That was what it seemed to do to her. She was a shadow of the person she'd been. The woman that had been able to keep the family together had receded to a place somewhere deep inside.

The spark that had lit that woman was nothing more than a simmering ember. Her depression consumed the fire that had lit her soul; the soul that had kept her family going, had faded, and yet they were still here. Her family was still here.

That was what it was really. Such a large part of her had been taken away, and it felt like Summer and Dave had really lost both of them that night, Aidan to the accident and Debbie to the depression. She was just not present, in any real sense. She had stopped engaging in life.

Thankfully, between the medication and ongoing therapy sessions, she was slowly coming out of her shell. She was starting to go out in public again, and she was eating better. As refreshing as those improvements were, she was nowhere near the woman she had been. That point, if ever to be reached again, was a long way off. For now, it was about the little improvements.

This had been harder than Dave ever imagined it could be. There was a time that they had really become cold to each other. They had both been so numb from the loss of Aidan, so self-absorbed with dealing with their own pain, that they were incapable of reaching out for each other. The sad thing was, that they both needed the comfort of each other.

You can't blame someone that's ill. Debbie was suffering from severe depression, and it wasn't her fault that he felt abandoned and lonely.

Well, yes, it was her fault in a way, and yes, he did blame her for him feeling lonely. The only problem with that logic was that it didn't help anyone. Having someone to blame doesn't take away the pain. It only allows frustration and hurt feelings to have a place to fester.

"I need some comfort. The nights are long and lonely. Tomorrow will be more of the same too. If only she would allow me to hold her. If only she would reach out to me, for comfort. We need to be together, to get through this. I am so tired of always being rejected. All it's doing, is adding to my pain. I have enough of that from the loss of Aidan."

He knew it would be easier to just stop trying and save himself from further rejection. He couldn't bring himself to do that, though. If he did, then he would surely lose his Debbie. That would be more than he could bear. Losing both of them, would be the end of him.

You know that's true! It tore you up when you lost them! These phantom thoughts had been coming to him more frequently. At first, he thought he was going insane. *Only sane people worry about going insane*, he told himself again. He supposed there was some truth in that, even if it was a delusional truth.

He found these thoughts easier to ignore, but he still didn't know where they came from. Since the accident he was having them more often. Maybe he needed to schedule an appointment with a psychologist.

Well, at least he had good people at the office that he could laugh with at times.

It was good to have something to look forward to. A warm smile can warm a cold heart.

Chapter 39

It always upset Summer, the way people looked at her and Tammy. What was their problem anyway? It wasn't like they had done anything wrong! The word spread around the school that they were dykes. So, of course, instantly they were both cast out. It didn't seem to matter whether there was any truth to the rumor. They'd been judged in the court of adolescent popular authority and had been found to be different. That was the worst possible offense to pubescent puritanism. Popularity was great! Athleticism, fantastic! Academic success was okay too. Diversity, however, was to be scrutinized, and more-often-than-not, rejected. A couple of lesbians in this small school was freakish. The way they figured it, and Summer heard it, was that if it wasn't true then why had neither of them dated any boys? Well, the idiots conveniently forgot about Shawn. If they did remember him, they justified him, then dismissed him in the same statement, "That was back in the sophomore year, it doesn't count!"

Well fuck all of 'em! It counted to her. Sophomore year still felt like yesterday. She lost her innocence the night Shawn threw away her love like so much trash. She still had her virginity, but not her innocence.

It was also the year she lost her brother. Two loves in such a short time ripped from her had left their scars. Add to that, living with the ghost of her mother. She was not the person she had been, and that hurt Summer like nothing else.

The truth was, that she and Tammy were very close, but not like that. No matter what everyone was saying, they were only very close friends.

"So, what's happening, girl?" Tammy asked as she arrived at Summer's locker.

"Nothing new. Everyone here looks at me like I'm an alien. Not like I give a shit!" Summer exploded. The fact was, she did care. While never exactly being in the popular crowd she had never been in the reject squad either. This was new territory for her. Last year people were still talking to her, they weren't whispering about her and giving her looks as she passed by. What had changed?

Since Aidan died, she'd retreated inside herself and didn't talk with people much. *Well, what would they do if they lost their brother?* she asked. People generally just gave her space. They didn't try to force her to talk. They just let her be.

Sandy had been there for her. She came over every day and held her and let her cry it out. She finally got Summer running again and in the end that was what kept her going. Well that, and the new friendship growing between her and Tammy. Sandy became jealous of her friendship with Tammy, saying there was something just not right with Tammy. Summer was convinced that she was just jealous of her choosing to spend time with Tammy instead of her, but Sandy started to come around less often. They barely even talked now. Sandy still told her about the rumors going around the school. One of the main ones was that Tammy was gay and people were starting to wonder about Summer too.

"People, or you, Sandy? If you want to know just ask me, why don't you?"

"Summer sweetie, you know I don't care one way or the other. You know we have been friends too long for this. I admit it, I am jealous of the time you are spending with her. We're best friends and we barely spend any time together anymore." Sandy reached out and took her hand. "I want my friend back."

Summer smiled at her and wrapped her arms around her. "I miss you too, you jealous bitch."

Sandy pulled back and inhaled so sharply Summer thought she was going to pass out. They both laughed themselves silly.

It felt good to have her friend back. Things went a little more back to what normal had been, but the rumors didn't stop. One day, a girl that was always trying to start a fight, was talking about her in front of the school, and a crowd of kids were around her, listening to the lies she was telling.

Summer had had enough. She walked right up to the girl and pushed her. Stacy was a good head taller than Summer. It didn't matter. Summer looked up into her face and said, "You are nothing but a homophobe! No, that isn't right. I don't think you even care enough to take a position one way or the other. I think all you care about is getting attention and making others feel worse than you do.

You keep on talking about Tammy. You've been talking about her for years now. She's a good person and she's my friend. She doesn't bother you. Why are you so fixated on her?"

"Because she's a freak bitch! Just like you." Stacy pushed Summer back. "What are you going to do? You are too pretty of a little bitch to do anything. What are you going to do? You gon'a call your dyke to protect you?" Stacy started laughing as she looked around at the faces in the crowd.

"It sounds like you're really fixated on Tammy. You sure do talk about lesbians a lot. I wonder why?"

Sandy's head whipped around, and hate radiated from her eyes.

Summer didn't give the bigger girl a chance. She punched her twice in the stomach and then wrapped her arm around her neck as she stepped forward. Stacy was bent over backwards, with her weight supported on Summer's knee across her back. There was no question that if Summer wanted to, she could apply pressure across Stacy's throat, cutting off her air supply.

"Are we done here?"

"Yeah, yeah, we're done. We're done, Stacy choked out the words in a whisper."

Summer had spent enough time wrestling with Aidan to have picked up a thing or three. She knew enough to let Stacy try to stand up from an off-balance position. As she predicted the bully tried to get in a cheap shot.

Summer had been waiting for it. She shot out her right leg and swept Sandy's legs out from under her using her. She then easily duck walked her knee into Stacy's gasping chest and grabbed a handful of hair lifting her head up off of the pavement.

"I thought we were done, Stacy. Did you want some more?"

The crowd burst out in laughter. Summer didn't take her eyes off Stacy. She saw her deflate. She was beat. Summer stood up and offered Stacy a hand up. She was too proud to take it.

"You and your dyke girlfriend can go and fuck yourselves!"

With that she had stormed off. That had been in the beginning of September and now Halloween was only days away. In that time, things had become worse and worse for her.

Oh well, Summer thought for the thousandth time. *School will be over soon and then off to college where I leave all of these small-minded people behind.*

She planned to go to UC Berkley like Aidan had planned. She was on track to be offered an academic full ride scholarship and was looking at what it would be like to live in a dorm. A lot of decisions to make. Until then, though, she had to get through high school, then this place could kiss her backside.

Chapter 40

Julie continued to drop by the house. Dave and Debbie really liked her, and it was easy to see why Aidan had fallen in love with her. This young woman was truly remarkable, a beautiful person.

Her beauty went way beyond her looks, of which she had plenty. She was genuine. There was no other way to say it. When she told you something, you could tell that she meant it. She was smart as well. They all enjoyed the time they spent together, usually in the kitchen. It really helped to bring all of them back together.

When Dave came home from work, he would usually prepare dinner. He had really refined his culinary skills and he enjoyed experimenting with different recipes. He liked tasting the rewards of his efforts, but it was the reassuring routine of making something, that he enjoyed. In this setting, he learned of the long friendship that Aidan and Julie had shared. She told him about the crush she had on him, before they both made their feelings known to each other.

He could tell, just from the way that she talked about him, how deep her love for Aidan went. Dave felt very good knowing that Julie was the mother of his granddaughter. Yes, she'd found out that she was having a little girl.

There were days when Debbie would join them. She'd usually sit at the table and talk with Julie, in the quiet voice she had adopted since she had started taking the medication. Sometimes, she would even join them in the cooking.

One special day, Summer and Julie were in the kitchen with Dave. They were making spaghetti with a clam sauce. Julie had made bruschetta and Summer was cutting the vegetables for a salad. Dave was leaning up against the counter, enjoying a glass of Merlot while the sauce simmered. Debbie came in and instead of sitting down at the table, she helped the girls to make the salad.

Dave was totally content watching these three beautiful women in his life interacting with each other. The fact they were doing something so every-day as making a salad together, gave the night such a satisfying feeling. It felt like a family was together. As simple a thing as that was, it was what had been missing in their home. There hadn't been a feeling of *family* in a long time.

Summer started to spend a lot of her time with Julie. Dave had no problem with that. He could see that they both were happier than they had been for quite some time and it was plain to see that they needed each other. He didn't think that it was only because of the loss that they both had suffered when Aidan died. And he didn't think it was only because of the baby growing inside Julie. He really thought that it was more than those two things. He believed it was because they needed something that the other had to offer. They really complemented each other. Now that's not to say that they always agreed with one another. He often heard them expressing their opposing views on everything, from whether they should have become involved in Iraq, to whether rap music was real music.

As time went on, it became obvious that all three women were filling a need that they had with each other. Somehow, by them interacting with each other, they were able to not only help each other, but to also draw the others out of themselves.

That's not to say that the relationship between Debbie and Dave magically improved. There was more going on between them than what could be blamed on the depression. No, there was something that had broken between them.

He had held out hope though. When he saw that Debbie was coming out of her shell, he allowed himself to hope that things between them could improve. He tried little things at first. He didn't want to push her, just sort of nudge her along, kind of scoot the momentum a bit in his direction. Well, that didn't work. At first, she was tolerant, but frosty. One time, he brought home flowers for all three of them. Summer and Julie raved about how thoughtful he was and gave him big dramatic hugs. Debbie, however, gave him a reluctant hug as she thanked him. He knew better than to have expected flowers would solve their problems in one fell swoop, but he hadn't expected her to respond with such coldness either. Needless to say, he was surprised and, to be honest, hurt by her reaction as well.

No matter how much he wanted to, he couldn't go back in time and make the accident not happen. Regardless of how many times he'd gone over and over the events that led up to that day, he knew he couldn't have prevented it.

At that moment Dave felt very clearly that Debbie was slipping away from him. He fought the feeling. He refused to let her go from him. If she slipped away, he knew that he couldn't face it.

No! I will not give up! I have to bring her back.

He knew he couldn't do anything to affect her depression. He couldn't just take it away from her. One of the hardest things for him to accept was that he could *not* fix this. This was something that Debbie had to do on her own. She would either come to terms with it, or it would consume her.

Chapter 41

They got the call early on a Tuesday morning that Julie was in labor. By the time they arrived at the hospital Julie had already finished the in-processing and was settled into her room. All that remained to do, was wait for the baby to let them know when it was time. As was expected, Julie's mother spent most of the time at her daughter's side.

Finally, a nurse arrived to update them on what was going on. "It's going to be a while still. Things are going fine. Julie's doing great. The doctor said it will be a few hours still." She looked around at the expectant faces. "The doctor has authorized access to the labor room." She smiled and led them through into the labor and delivery wing.

Julie looked like she was doing well. She had a better grip on the situation than the women that had been through the process before. After standing around for a while Dave realized that he was little more than wall-dressing. He kissed Julie on the forehead and let her know that he was going to wait outside.

"Holler if you need me," he said to her with smiling broadly. He winked and gave her hand a reassuring squeeze. She squeezed his hand back.

"I'm pretty sure that I'm going to be hollering quite a bit in a little while."

He put both of his strong hands around hers. He could see the fear on her face.

"You're going to be just fine. You are strong. I love you, sweetheart." Dave reached out and put his hand on Julie's father's shoulder and pulled him over to take his spot next to his daughter's side. Dave backed out of the room and made his way back to the waiting room. The women didn't even glance at him as he left the room. They were in full assist mode.

Dave had too much pent-up energy to sit still for long. He walked along the halls and eventually found that he had wandered back to the waiting room. *There was more than enough support and suggestions in that room*, he thought to himself.

He felt more than a little useless. That brought a smile to his face. It was just the way he'd felt when his own children were making their way into the world. The difference was, that he was at Debbie's side when both Aidan and Summer were born. As much as he loved Julie, she wasn't his daughter, and as competent as Dave was in most situations, he readily conceded his ineptitude in this situation.

A little while later Anne, Julie's mother, joined him. Other than a few words at Aidan's funeral they hadn't spoken more than ten words to each other. In time, Anne looked at Dave and said, "I want to thank you. Over the past few weeks Julie has found a sense of peace. I know a big reason for that is because you accepted her as a member of your family."

He could tell she was close to crying. He slowly stood and crossed the six steps that separated them. He knelt down onto the worn industrial carpeting in front of her and took her hand in his.

"Anne", he said looking her full in the face, "Julie is a member of our family, so are you. That child she's bringing into this world is a part of us. That child is my first grandchild." A small smile tugged at the corners of his mouth. "Your daughter is a very special person. I know that if Aidan hadn't been taken from us, they would have had a great marriage. Anne, all I can say is that we are family and I am glad that we are. I know that they were not married, but I feel like she is a daughter none-the-less."

Anne nodded her head as the tears fell down her cheeks. They stayed like that for some time. Dave didn't know how long, but eventually he had to stand up. His knees hurt too much to keep on kneeling. One more reminder that today he was becoming a grandfather.

After 17 hours of labor little Aida Marie Thompson arrived into the world. Mother and baby were doing great.

Every parent and Grandparent says that the baby is beautiful, but in this case, it was true. Little Aida Marie was a beautiful baby. She had big alert eyes that seemed to be taking in everything at once and all the while she had this cute little half smile on her face. Okay, maybe the smile was only a sign of gas, but it was adorable anyway.

Julie stayed a part of their everyday lives and they were able to watch as Aida learned to crawl and then as she took her first hesitant steps in the kitchen. The hesitation didn't last long as she was soon running all over the house. She was a breath of life in their home.

Debbie slowly came out of her depression. The therapy and medication had obviously done their job. Dave credited a big part of her recovery to Debbie wanting to live again. She saw a reason to engage with life again and held on for dear life. Things didn't instantly return to normal. By no stretch of the imagination were they normal, but their relationship had become more tolerant of each other. It was comfortable. They had reconciled their differences. They had come back together across a very dark void.

Chapter 42

It was a nice summer day. Julie and Debbie were in the back yard playing with the baby. There was a nice breeze blowing, just enough to keep the heat from the sun from being too much. Aida was busy digging in the dirt. As much as Julie tried to keep her clean, Aida was not that type of child. She was at her happiest with her shoes off and dirt under her nails. In this, she was like her dad.

Aidan had driven Debbie crazy by doing the same things as a baby. With Aida, Debbie just smiled and tried to re-assure Julie that Aida would be just fine, even if she did occasionally crunch on the wayward ant or worm.

After Aida woke up from her nap Dave broke out the barbecue grill. Debbie had been marinating the meat for the kebabs since yesterday and he had some sausages to go with them, as well as some cheese-dogs for Aida.

Julie's mother, Anne, joined them for dinner, along with a couple of neighbors.

Summer did a typical teenage fly-through. She arrived home just as dinner was ready, scarfed down her food, then said she had to run. Well, it was nice of her to take time out of her busy schedule to join them.

The next morning, Dave woke to something that he hadn't experienced in a long time. The first thing he noticed was that there was music playing. Summer didn't usually turn her music on until after breakfast. The next thing that struck him was the smell of bacon and eggs cooking. Curious, he made his way to the kitchen. Debbie was busy at the stove, cooking away. Dave just leaned against the doorframe and watched her go about the task of preparing breakfast. She paused for a moment and took a drink from her coffee. She put it down and then turned and started walking to the fridge. Startled, she stopped short with her hand over her heart!

"Dave, you scared me!"

"I'm sorry, I didn't want to break the mood. It looked like you were enjoying yourself and I didn't want to break that up."

"Well, there's no need to worry about that. Get your butt in here and help me, will ya? You can get the oranges out and start squeezing them. Princess sleepy head should be waking up any time now. Oh, and good morning." She surprised him by stepping up to him and planting a kiss on his surprised lips.

"Good morning to you too." Dave unsuccessfully tried to hide his surprise.

"Dave, it has been too long since we have said good morning to each other. Things need to change. In fact, how would you like to go out on a date with me tonight?"

He was glad she had asked him with her back to him. That way, she couldn't see the surprised look on his face. He tried to imagine where this was coming from. He didn't have a clue or, for that matter, a care.

Before Debbie took his hesitation for reluctance on his part he said, "That sounds like a good idea, a very good idea. Is there someplace you would like to go?"

"Actually, there is, I'll take care of the reservations. Is seven good for you?"

"Sure, what's the dress code?" he asked jokingly.

"Let's do semi-formal. Your grey suit would be perfect."

"Ok, a date it is." Dave was surprised to find that he was nervous. Nervous about taking his wife of twenty years on a date? Then it hit him. He wasn't nervous about the date. He was nervous about the reason for the date. Would this be a try at a new beginning or another false start? Either way at the end of the night he would have a better idea.

He was sitting in the living room watching the news when Debbie came down the stairs. He'd forgotten just how beautiful a woman she was. She had on a blue dress that really made her curves stand out, while somehow leaving enough to the imagination, to be provocative. She looked beautiful and he wasted no time in telling her so.

She gave a curtsey and said, "Well thank you, sir. Now kindly pick your tongue off the floor, before you leave a spot on the carpet."

That was when he looked up at the landing on the stairs. Summer was standing there with a smile on her face. He gave her a wink.

"Excuse me, my love. I'll be right back." He went into the kitchen to get the roses he'd bought earlier. He still didn't know what direction this night was going to take, but so far it was starting off nicely.

Summer gave both of her parents a kiss. "Have my mom home by eleven or you'll be in trouble mister," she said, wagging her finger at her dad.

"My intentions are completely honorable, miss, he said giving her a small bow.

Once they were in the car, he looked at Debbie and asked her "Where to?"

She decided to keep him in suspense by giving him turn by turn directions. They eventually led them to one of the best restaurants in town. *The Fish Shack* didn't sound like much, but it was usually impossible to find a table on any night of the week. Debbie had either been very lucky, or she had planned this for some time. Well, either way was fine by him. He wanted to enjoy this night and she obviously did too.

The meal was fantastic! The conversation was not quite as good. For some reason, well, for many reasons they were not talking about, they were awkward with each other. They were both making an effort, but it was strained. By the time they got to dessert they had settled into a quiet pause. They shared a tort and then had an espresso.

Dave reflected on the night as he drove them home. He was sure that she was doing the same. Kind of funny that he was going over in his mind what had happened, instead of talking with her. She was sitting right next to him. Sitting right there and looking completely gorgeous. The love of his life, right there in the passenger seat, and it felt like she was a long way away.

It was obvious she was trying to become closer. He was happy that she was willing to try, and he was going to do his best to do the same. Instead of going home, Dave drove to a quiet spot and parked the car.

"Dave Thompson, are you trying to take me parking with you? I'll have you know that I am a good girl," she said crossing her arms across her chest.

"Oh, I know you're a good girl. In fact, I know you are wonderful, smart, gorgeous, and worth far more than I could ever give you." He looked her directly in the eye. "Debbie, I love you. I've always loved you and I always will. You are everything to me."

She leaned into him and met him half way.

Later, Dave opened the door for her as they walked into the kitchen. They tried to be quiet. They didn't want to wake up Summer.

"Do you want another cup of coffee, or maybe a nightcap?" Dave asked her in a whisper.

"Actually, a glass of wine sounds good."

"Do you have any preference?"

"There's a bottle of Pinot in the fridge."

She had really thought this night through. He wondered if it had been going as she had planned. Maybe she was just playing it by ear at this point. Either way, this was a better night than either one of them had had for a very long time.

When he returned with wine in hand, he found that she had moved into the living room and was sitting on the couch. She was sitting on her foot looking incredibly sexy.

"Here, have a seat," she said as she patted the cushion next to her.

He did as she asked and went to work on un-corking the wine and pouring them each a glass.

"Do you mind?" she asked him as she looked at his lap.

"No, please do," he said with a big smile.

Debbie had always liked stretching her legs out onto his lap. It never failed, when she did, he would rub her legs and feet. Tonight, was no exception. He went right into the old habit. Debbie took a sip of wine and closed her eyes. She leaned back into the couch and let out a long breath. "That's nice."

He couldn't agree more, it was nice. And not just the fact that he was rubbing her sexy legs. This whole mood was nice. What was better, was that it didn't feel strained. It felt good.

Unfortunately for his raging libido, Debbie didn't give any signs that she was interested in anything more. He knew better than to push his good fortune, so he took comfort in what they had enjoyed.

In time, Debbie pulled her feet off his lap, and stood up. She lost her balance a little bit.

Dave jumped up to steady her. "I have you," he said as they found themselves only inches apart and staring into each other's eyes. Debbie closed hers and leaned into him. They kissed, tentatively at first, but it shortly turned into a deeper kiss. Debbie all of a sudden, broke contact and looked up into his face.

Having made her decision, she took her husband by the hand and led him up to their bed.

Chapter 43

The State Police Cruiser slowed to a stop, the gravel on the side of the road crunched under the weight of its tires. Officer Michaels shook his head as he looked at the smashed guardrail. He knew the vehicle that left these skid-marks, was lying broken, somewhere below, in the rocky ravine. He was very familiar with this curve in the road. Three years ago, a car full of kids died after going over the edge.

He put his hands on his utility belt and let out a tired sigh as he took in the scene below him. He saw a small section of the roof of the mostly submerged car. It was barely visible through the trees.

Pulling out his radio, he called in the accident.

"Dispatch, this is Mike Bravo 24."

"Go Mike Bravo 24."

"Dispatch, we have a single vehicle accident on SR 267 north, at marker mile marker 46, request two additional units, ambulance, and mountain extraction team."

The mountain extraction teams were trained for these kinds of accidents and, unfortunately, also had a lot of real-world experience. At least one thing was in their favor—it wasn't even noon yet, so they had plenty of daylight to work with. Officer Michaels went to the back of the cruiser to get his rappelling gear out of the trunk. He finished cinching into his rig and then secured his line to a stable post of the guardrail. He hoped it just might help to save someone's life after all. He paused, at the edge of the precipice, and went over his mental check-list one final time, before committing to the descent. Instead of easing his weight into his rig, he went back to the trunk of his cruiser and grabbed some thermal blankets.

With the blankets secured, he mentally prepared himself before stepping over the edge. He knew from experience how treacherous it was to go down this side of the mountain. He reflected on the discovery he'd made the last time he made this trip. Maybe this time he would be able to do more than clean up the mess. He sent up a silent prayer for a better ending.

"Focus," he said to himself. "If you lose it, you are no good to whoever is down there that needs you. One step at a time, just keep it steady." He steeled himself. "Here goes nothing."

Dave sat up in bed with an urgent need to relieve himself. He stumbled out of bed and made his way to the bathroom.

What a crazy dream. Standing over the toilet he let his mind wander. He realized he knew the place he'd been dreaming about. It was on the way to Debbie's parent's lake house. He shook his head as he finished his business.

His subconscious must have dredged up the memory of him reading about the accident when that car full of kids had crashed and died in the cold waters of the river.

Dave had an involuntary shiver as his body went frigid. He stopped in his tracks and took a deep breath. The cold feeling went away as quickly as it had come over him.

He crawled back under his warm covers and put a hand on Debbie's shoulder. He needed to touch her, he needed to feel that she was there with him.

Sometime later he was able to drift back into a thin sleep, but he was troubled with more disturbing dreams.

Chapter 44

He felt a comfortable heat on his face and heard the comfortable sound of a crackling fire. He knew he was sitting in a chair, facing the fire. He realized he wasn't alone. He was sitting in a room with other people. They moved around him, but they were nothing more than hazy shapes to him, forms without substance, out of focus. Their voices were like the grinding sound of the surf. He sat there with the heat on his face and their murmuring washing over him. None of it mattered to him. This wasn't real, he was just dreaming again.

He realized that a woman was talking to him. Her voice was fuzzy, distant. It sounded like she was talking to him through a wall. He tried to focus on her words but couldn't bring himself to do it. He felt like he was drifting away. His body didn't weigh anything. He let himself go and drifted away.

"I thought I might find you here."

Dave looked around and realized he was once more on the side of the road. Debbie was sitting on the guardrail, a beautiful smile on her face.

"I knew you'd come back."

"Why are we here, Debbie?" he asked her, looking around.

"You know why, Dave. You remember."

The events leading up to that day went through his mind like an old 8 mm movie, the frames rapidly clicking by. He knew that it was his decisions which had led them to what had happened.

If he had been more focused on his family, instead of work, then he would have been home instead of working late. He would have been well rested and wouldn't have fallen asleep, behind the wheel. He wouldn't have put their lives at risk.

I almost killed them all, he thought.

You DID kill them!

Where had that thought come from? Along with it came the most heart wrenching sadness he'd ever felt. Tears streamed down his cheeks. His whole body was wracked with uncontrollable sobs. He let it wash over him.

He sat down on the shoulder of the road with his back leaning against the guardrail post. Once his tears started to slow, his vision cleared enough for him to look down the side of the mountain, at the scar their crash had left. He saw the tree they crashed into, right after leaving the road. It was a thick, solid tree up to the point it ended in jagged splinters. Luckily, their journey had ended in a shallow part of the stream. The water had built up rock and flotsam, due to the curve in its course, as it followed the contour of the mountain. This had created an extension of the bank, that had kept the car from going completely under. If they had landed ten feet in either direction, they would have surely drowned.

He thought about trying to climb down to the stream, so he could look at the place the car had come to rest, but decided it wasn't worth risking breaking his neck in the process. He'd been lucky on this mountain once, he wasn't going to give it another chance for his stupidity to get the best of him.

"Dave, you know what happened, what really happened. You need to open your eyes. Dave! Open your eyes!"

"Dave, LOOK AT THE ROAD!" Debbie's voice cut through the fog.

"DAD!" Aidan screamed at the top of his lungs.

His eyes shot open. They were about to go off the road. They were going to miss the guardrail by a good five feet. They weren't even going to be slowed down by that before going over the edge.

He slammed on the brakes and pulled the wheel, as hard as he could to the left. He knew it was already far too late. The car skidded on the road with the wheels locked up. The tires screamed in protest, his children and wife's screams blended in with his own as they flew over the edge.

He sent a desperate prayer to heaven that somehow everyone would be okay. The car slammed into a tree with the right rear quarter panel, spinning the car to the right. Debbie's side slammed into another tree. Luckily the car didn't flip over, but landed on its wheels, two of which immediately exploded. The sound of the car smashing a path down the mountain mixed with their desperate cries was deafening. They slammed into trees and boulders as the car careened completely out of control down the steep hillside, gouging a path of destruction along the way.

On a branch of a tree, Dave clearly saw a raccoon looking at them as they invaded his previously serene afternoon. It was as if time slowed down as their beat-up car raced past him. Dave could see crumbs on the fur around his muzzle from what looked like a piece of bread he held in his tiny paws. Then, all-of-a-sudden, he saw a dark shape jump out at him from the left. The car slammed into what must have been a very large tree. Everything lurched hard to the left. He felt an incredible pressure all down his left side then everything blacked out.

"DAD! HELP ME!! The water's coming in! DAD, HELP ME!" The door won't open." He heard Aidan banging his shoulder against the door, trying in vain to force it open. "I can't open the window. DAD Wake UP!" Aidan yelled at him.

Dave heard him straining to get out.

Dave tried to turn around to see what he was talking about.

How could water be coming in? He couldn't turn his head. He couldn't even move his arms. Everything felt fuzzy around the edges. *That's strange*, he thought. No matter how hard he tried he couldn't open his eyes.

He could hear Aidan screaming for him to help him.

He felt the cold water creeping up his legs. He must have blacked out because the next thing he realized was that the water had reached his chest.

He realized Aidan wasn't screaming. He felt a surge at that thought. He thought that it was strange that he had not heard Summer or Debbie at all.

It was complete silence except for the lapping of the cold water as it rose up his body. He knew he was in trouble when it reached his chin.

"Debbie?" He tried to reach out his hand to touch her. He fought to open his eyes and managed to crack them open enough to see that the car was tilted to the right. His hand floated in the water. He concentrated on reaching out to Debbie. His hand wasn't moving.

"Summer, honey, are you okay baby?" Dave's voice hitched. "Summer baby, tell me you're okay."

"Aidan, son, are you still with me? Aidan? … No!"

He knew, even as his mind was railing against the situation, that he was only yelling inside his own head. He couldn't keep his eyes open.

Everything was cold and dark.

Everything was slipping away as the cold settled into his soul and carried him away.

Chapter 45

The rain fell from the heavy gray sky. It made a shushing sound as it bounced off the windows. The old man was sitting in a wheelchair facing the windows, a plaid red blanket covered his legs to keep them warm. As usual, he had his eyes closed and looked like he was dreaming. The fire was crackling in the fireplace. The sound of the rain and the crackling fire gave a cozy feeling to what was usually a drab and cheerless room.

Chantal looked at him kindly. Dave was still her favorite, after all these years. He had patiently listened to her as she told him all about her life, the good times and the bad.

She had helped him when he had bad days. She'd been there to help calm him down and took care of cleaning up the messes he made. Not that he had many bad days over the last few years. He was gone a lot more than he was here.

Dave was at home. *Where's home?* He quickly threw away the distracting thought. Over the years he had become very good at disregarding reality, so he could focus on his own reality.

He was sitting on the lawn-swing in his backyard. He let the warm feeling of the whisky he was sipping, warm the parts of him that were so cold.

A wind was picking up. He heard it as it whistled through the branches of the spruce trees lining the back of the yard. The gentle bubbling of the water as it flowed into the pond, mixed with the cooling breeze, helped him relax. The whisky was beginning to help take the edge off his pain as well.

He took a deep breath and slouched down in the lawn swing and looked up to the stars above. He sat there for a while without thinking about anything, just letting his mind wander. He didn't want to think about any of his problems. All he wanted to do was to feel relaxed.

Sometime later, he heard the back door open and then gently close. He didn't take his eyes off the stars as he felt a weight settle down next to him.

"Do you remember when you used to show me where the constellations were, Daddy?"

"I sure do, baby girl. It's one of the best memories I have."

"Mine too, Daddy." Summer wrapped her arm in his and snuggled into her father.

"I feel so tired. Life is so hard sometimes, baby." He closed his eyes and thought about how things used to be. How much simpler things had been?

He felt a couple of raindrops land on his face as they started to fall from the sky. He could still see the stars, but the clouds were steadily moving in.

"I'm so tired," he declared with a long sigh.

"Are you ready to go, Daddy?" Summer asked him. She didn't raise her head from his chest. She didn't think he was ready, but she asked anyway, more as a suggestion.

"Not yet, baby girl. I want to stay a little longer. You know things didn't always seem so complicated. There was a time when I had it all figured out, you know?"

"Tell me, Daddy."

"I had you, Aidan, and your mom, and we had love. Do you remember, Summer, when we would all just turn up the radio in the kitchen? I would make pancakes on Saturday mornings, and we would just dance to the music? Remember when we just had fun together?" he asked her. "We haven't danced like that in a long time. I'm so sorry baby girl, you deserve better."

"It's okay, daddy, I love you. We all do. … Are you ready to go now?" she asked him.

"No, honey, not quite yet, I think I'll stay for just a little longer."

Chantal was going around and checking her patients. She came over to Dave and adjusted the blanket on his legs.

She noticed a smile spread across his old, tired face. Not just an ordinary smile either. It was a real jaw cracker. In all the time she had cared for Dave, she'd never seen him look so happy.

"That's good, my lovely man. You deserve to feel happy!" she told him.

Tears were leaking from the corners of his eyes. She reached down to his weathered face and gently brushed them away. That's when she heard him say, "I'm ready to go now, baby girl."

Dave slowly raised his head and saw Summer was looking up at him with a big smile on her ten-year-old face.

He lifted his gaze higher and looked over Summer's shoulder. Aidan and Debbie were standing by the door beside the fireplace.

The light that was coming down from the old fluorescent bulbs didn't do much to push away the gray light coming in through the windows.

The storm was a gentle one. Dave always liked rainy days. They washed away all the grime and left the world fresh and new. This was no exception. It was a gentle cleansing rain that was coming down.

Out of the corner of his eye, Dave saw Chantal smiling at him.

For a moment Dave was confused. *This is strange.* He thought. *Chantal and Debbie here? Chantal is younger than Debbie, isn't she?* Too many questions that did not matter anymore.

"Daddy are you ready to come home?"

Dave looked down into the beautiful face of his daughter. She took his hand and supported his arm. She helped him stand up from the chair. He felt strength flowing into him, a strength he hadn't felt in years. He stood up to his full height, straight and tall, and took the first, confident, step to meet his wife and son. They were both standing with their arms outstretched, welcoming him into their embrace. He closed the distance with tears streaming down his face. With each step he took, the years slipped off him. His pace picked up, the closer he came to his family, the family that he was so sure he would never see again.

They reached out their hands to him as they seemed to get a little brighter.

Chantal put her finger under Dave's nose, to feel if he was still breathing. His face had relaxed, and she didn't see his chest rising and falling anymore.

I'm coming home, my loves.

The End

Afterword

Thank you, dear reader, for taking this journey with me. I hope you have enjoyed reading A Life Worth Living as much as I enjoyed writing it.

The idea for this story came to me while I was driving with my family on a trip to see relatives. My mind was able to wander a bit while driving mile after mile down the highway. As the story began to develop, during that drive, I felt that it was a story that needed to be told. I have to admit that my time with the relatives during that vacation was limited as I was engrossed with giving life to these wonderful characters. Thank you for bearing with me along the way. This story is my first novel length work and I have learned a lot along the way. I hope you forgive my stumbling's. It is my sincere desire that by sharing these characters with you maybe some of these lessons will come in handy for you. A wise friend of mine once told me "No one has ever lain on their death bed and wished that they had spent more time at work." These words I have tried to embrace. I do believe that working hard is essential to having a good life. However, as with all things, a balance must be kept. In life there are precious moments that you are either there for or you are not. There is no going back and editing the page. Life moves on and we have to live with the decisions we make. In the end I only hope that we all can look back and say that we have made ours A Life Worth Living.

With that said, it is my sincere hope that you have enjoyed taking this journey with me and I look forward to sharing the next one with you soon.

I am working on my next book titled Fault line. Watch for it to come out in 2015.

Thank you for your support.

T. L. Scott

23 November 2014

Excerpt

Fault Line

Chapter 1

Late summer is a wonderful time of year. The sun has eased back from the blistering intensity of July. It now warms the skin instead of frying it like an egg in a skillet. The air has lost some of its sweltering quality. A cool breeze stirs the air and then rolls gently through the park.

This green oasis of nature is a favorite place for kids of all ages. People play catch with Frisbees, while others toss a baseball back and forth. Tired mothers stand at the ready, keeping a watchful eye on their tireless toddlers at play. Young couples lay on blankets, basking in the sun as much as they are basking in their love. People feed the ducks by the pond. Joggers make their way along the path which winds around the promenade and continues on its serpentine route through the park. The rhythmic cadence of their footfalls add to the natural rhythm of the day. At the south-eastern corner, a black lab races along the green expanse of grass and launches into the air to catch a Frisbee with effortless grace.

Bill is taking it all in. It feels good to be back home. The smell of fresh-cut grass combined with the morning breeze helps him to relax like he hasn’t been able to do for so long.

"Man, you gotta get the Shelby. If you're going to get a Mustang, you might as well get the best," said Sam. He was from Virginia Beach and had grown up around muscle cars. His dad taught him some of life's most valuable lessons while tinkering under the hood of one project after another. When it came to cars, Sam knew what he was talking about. His favorite project had been rebuilding a 442 with his dad and uncle. It was the first time his dad had involved him in the restoration of the engine and transmission. Before that, he'd mostly done body work and been the one to fetch what the men needed. In fact, looking back, it was that restoration more than anything else which had led him to decide on being a 63B, light vehicle mechanic.

"Listen, man," said Sebastian, "I still haven't made up my mind. Yeah, I love the Shelby, but that Camaro is awesome too." He held up his hands to forestall the complaints he knew were coming.

"Before you say that it can't compare with the Mustang, think about after-market work. With some fine tuning and a little tweak to the computer chip, she'd be sweet! Now toss in a new transmission, and it would scream!" Sebastian was an Army brat and had spent most of his childhood in Germany. He had always been good with electronics and had initially come into the Army to do that. Once he was in the Army, he learned about the things the guys in EOD did so he cross-trained and became an 89D.

"It still wouldn't be the same," grumbled Sam.

"To tell you the truth, I'm leaning toward the Beamer. I've been reading about the M3, and it's a complete package. I like the way it rides so low to the ground. It really hugs the road." Sebastian scooted to the edge of his chair while he was talking. "It's got 425 horsepower pushing around 4,000 pounds. Get this man, it goes zero to sixty in four-point-five seconds!"

"Your right man," said Tommy, "that M3 is sweet." He was leaning back as usual. His pose and attitude, as usual, was relaxed. "For me though, I'm going to get a Range Rover."

Tommy was from Atlanta and would be going there to visit his mother after the wedding. Like the rest of the guys, he hadn't been home in over eight months. He was an only child and in-spite-of his tough exterior, he had a soft spot for his mother. She had made a lot of sacrifices for him. His dad died when he was young, and she'd raised him as a single mother. He owed her a lot and tried to respect her sacrifices by becoming the best man he could be. He had big shoes to fill. His father had been a great man. Tommy constantly strove to become better. One day maybe someone would think that he'd been a great man as well.

"You're all crazy," said Raul. "The classics are the best. I'm gonna get me a '78 Monte Carlo and trick it out. Picture it man, lime green, chrome rims, at least 32's, and full hydraulics, a true hopper." He crossed his arms and sat back with a smug look on his face. When none of the guys showed any reaction, he quickly sat forward on his chair again and put his hands on his knees.

"You've got to be shittin' me guys. You don't know what a hopper is?" He held his hand out, palm down, and bounced it up and down, small at first then bigger and bigger. "Sweet right?" he asked, leaning back again with a big smile.

Raul was a proud New Yorker. As much as he loved his city, he knew he had to leave her to find himself. He'd seen too many friends die over stupid things. He wasn't afraid to die. Dying was easy, he wanted to make something of himself. That was hard. He had to work at it all the time.

He knew what he needed to do the first time he heard a presentation by an Army recruiter. He'd never been good at school. He wasn't bad at it; he was a C student. He just wasn't interested in what they were teaching him.

Most of his teachers tried about as hard as the kids. Everybody was coasting through. School was a place he had to go to so he could get out of there. He knew that drop-outs never got away. He had to finish High School so he could get away and make a difference. The Army needed soldiers. It turned out to be a good match.

Once he enlisted, he decided he liked the camaraderie and worked hard to become better. He graduated at or near the top of his classes. He found that he liked to learn. It was different than school back at home. This was stuff he wanted to know. The instructors really cared about teaching you. They got up close and personal. The lessons were going to keep him and his buddies alive. He decided to try some college classes after he settled into his first posting at Fort Bragg. He finished his Bachelor's degree in three years and was working on his Masters in Adverse Psychology. Along the way, he also completed Army Sniper training. He had a real knack for observing and analyzing. He was also very good at taking action, when it was the right time.

Bill sat back and listened. He was usually the quiet one of the group. These were his friends, and he knew he was damn lucky to have them. It was funny that two years ago they hadn't known each other. They came from different walks of life. Each man had decided to join for his own reasons. At the core of it, they were looking for the same thing. Each of them wanted to become better than what they were. They'd become as close as any brothers. Being in battle together does that; especially when they'd saved each other's lives too many times to count.

Bill watched the tranquil scene of normal life play out in the park across the street. A large, black crow was working on a crust of bread. It would attack the prize a few times with its beak, then raise its head, darting it from side to side to make sure his perimeter was clear. The crow was cautious. He made sure his prize was still safely his. Satisfied, it returned its attention to the bread, stabbing its beak into the crusty morsel. Suddenly, it dropped the meal and launched into the air.

The unmistakable crack of a gunshot shattered the tranquility.

Instinct and experience guided Bill's eyes over his left shoulder. Reflex and muscle training guided him as he gracefully turned his body, rising fluidly off the chair, his eyes searching for the aggressor. He dropped to a kneeling position to minimize his exposure to the potential aggressor. His right knee hadn't made contact with the red bricks of the patio before his eyes locked on the target. His right hand clasped the grip of his Sig Sauer SP 2022 Nitron. Having identified his target, he began clearing it from the holster. His left arm, now clear of the seatback, came around for a two-handed grip. His sights locked on the confirmed threat.

A man stood over a woman in the middle of the two-lane road. She was down on her knees, gesturing with her hands fiercely. Bill couldn't make out the words they were saying from this distance, but it was obvious he wasn't asking her out on a date. The man was holding the stock of what looked like an AK 47 with his right hand, waving it around menacingly, while shouting at the woman. His long, stringy, brown hair whipped around his head. He punctuated his agitation by thrusting the gun up and down.

The woman raised up off her heels and said something. Whatever she said caught his attention. He closed the distance between them then bent his thin frame down so his face was inches from hers.

She shrank back from his leering face. Whatever it was she said next, he must have found amusing. He tossed his head back and laughed, then started dancing around her. He was doing a kind of high-step, his knees pumping high while he jabbed the rifle sharply up and down. He was really getting it too. He completed his circle of her and stomped his heavy boot down, ending his dance. He threw his head back and howled like a wolf. Bill had to give it to him; the guy had some good lungs.

The man took in a deep breath as he rolled his body back forward. He snugged the butt of the gun into his shoulder and sighted in on the woman. The black barrel ended inches from her upturned face. Her jet-black hair blew back from her face in the gentle breeze. It, and the angle she was facing prevented Bill from seeing her face.

Bill admired the way she faced the man that was about to take her life. She looked proud and strong. Even if she was seconds from meeting her maker, she wasn't going to cower. He respected her for that.

Bill increased the pressure of his trigger finger. Seeing the man tense his shoulder and bring his right elbow out to the side triggered Bill to engage fully. A split second before applying the final amount of pressure, the dancer jerked to the right. He fell in what seemed like slow motion, Bill knew better it was what he called battle speed. Bullets sprayed out from the barrel of the AK47 in a deadly arc. It was good that the rifle shot up to six hundred rounds-per-minute. It quickly ran out of ammo before anyone was hurt by this madman. With the guy out of the fight, Bill scanned for more threats. Seeing none, he did a quick check on his friends. Sam and Raul were both covering down on the baddie.

Bill kept his weapon trained on the inert form in the road, from his kneeling position. He cut his eyes over to Tommy and Sebastian and saw they were taking cover behind the decorative fence that separated the café from the sidewalk. He could see they were at a loss. They were used to being in uniform and reacting as they were trained to do. When their finely-honed reactions came up with a missing weapon, they didn't have an answer for a beat. This wasn't Iraq or Afghanistan; it was Texas, and yet war had found them here.

Bill kept his weapon pointed at the bad guy as he ran over to the woman. She was still on her knees in the middle of the road. The man hadn't moved since he'd hit the pavement. Bill saw why. A pool of blood spread out from his head. The blood looked black on the asphalt road. A smaller puddle was congealing under his torso as well. Bill wasn't taking any chances. He'd seen men get up from wounds that should've killed them outright before.

He slowly circled the body, keeping his eyes on the man's hands. If they so much as twitched, Bill would drop the hammer. His finger skillfully had four of the seven pounds of pressure squeezing the match grade trigger. It would only take a small fraction more to dispatch the man if needed. He kicked the rifle away from the corpse and then looked at the woman. She was staring at the body.

Bill couldn't see her face from his angle. Her black hair was loose and partially covered it. He could see that she was shivering in-spite-of the warm air.

A crowd was beginning to form. Sam and Raul were still training their weapons around, searching for any more potential threats. Sebastian and Tommy were keeping the small crowd that had formed back, maintaining a loose perimeter defense. They were doing their best to keep the look-e-loos away from the scene. Of course, in this modern day, most of the people had their phones out, trying to catch it all on video. It would be up on social media before the authorities had a chance to arrive on the scene.

"Are you okay ma'am?"

She raised her obsidian eyes to his and said in a calm voice, "I think so."

"Are you hurt?" Bill asked her.

"No, . . . I don't think so," she replied shaking her head slowly.

"Are there any more of them?" He asked as he cast his eyes around.

"I don't know," answered the woman. "I don't know who he is."

She looked down at her lap, and her body sagged down. The steel that had held her up seemed to leave her. "He was really going to kill me," she murmured.

They both knew she'd spoken the truth. Bill didn't see any need to say anything further on that point.

"What's your name ma'am?" He asked her in a gentle tone as he reached out his hand to help her up.

She took it and let him help her to her feet. Once she was sure she wasn't going to fall back down, she squeezed his hand a little and responded; "My name is Isabella, thank you." She said looking him in the eye.

"You're welcome," he replied simply.

There was something about this woman, something more than her beauty. There was a feeling of strength that radiated from her. He tore his gaze from her beautiful eyes and looked around at the scene developing around them.

More people had gathered on the sidewalks on both sides of the street. Traffic was at a standstill. Cars were lined up with their doors standing open. Their drivers had abandoned them to get a better look at the aftermath of the violence that had played out in their small town. Small children were standing with their parents. Some parents were trying to cover their children's eyes, but the curious little ones weren't having it. Bill wished he could cover the body up. Not to give the man his dignity but to lessen the macabre interest that had overtaken these people. He knew better though; he knew the police were going to conduct an investigation. Back here, that meant collecting forensic evidence. As if on cue, the shrill notes of a siren cut through the still morning air. Altogether, less than three minutes had passed since the first shot had been fired, and the discordant wail sounded the arrival of law and order.

Chapter 2

In the time it took for that terrible scene to play out, on what ironically was Main Street, the crow had made it to the edge of the small town, and a very bad man knew that things had changed.

Sound travels well over the dry air. To a trained ear there is no mistaking the crack of a rifle. When a person was as experienced with weapons as this particular man was, they can even tell the type of rifle fired.

He knew the sound had likely come from one of his men. The wind whispered the story into his well-trained ear. The answering report of pistols told the next chapter. It was the ensuing silence which told him the conclusion of this drama had played out. His man was probably dead. If not dead, then he would soon be locked up in a jail cell. Regardless, the heat had just been cranked up several degrees.

The warehouse he was standing in was far enough from the road that it avoided attention and was still close enough for quick transportation of the goods he traded in. It had proved to be a good place for a temporary headquarters. It had hills on three sides with the front opening out to the road in the distance. The road leading into it wound down into this valley. The warehouse had been built up, so it sat higher than the ground around it to prevent the products stored inside getting damaged during the few times it rained heavily.

He looked out at the gravel road which cut its way out to highway 27. His eye caught the movement of a single bird. It flew, rising on the air that was heating as the sun cut higher into the sky. He stood in the entrance to the warehouse for a few minutes, just letting his eyes and thoughts wander. In time, he saw a cloud of dust rising from the gravel road.

“Have him brought up to the office,” he said to his men that were stationed on each side of the door, their weapons at the ready.

He made his way to the east side of the building and looked over his operation as he went. A group of his men was loosely gathered by the trucks. Some of them were working on the engines, but most were just standing around and talking. Another group was gathered around the cages on the other side of the building. He heard some tell-tale sounds coming from the smaller administrative offices. He didn't care if the men had some fun, as long as they didn't damage the product.

Everything seemed to be under control. He climbed the metal stairs to the office, noting the positions of the guards that were up on the rafters. One of the men noticed him and gave a small wave. Miguel forced a smile on his hard face and returned the salute. He had learned over time that some men responded better if there was a sense of camaraderie. All Miguel cared about was that the men did what he told them to and were loyal. Whatever it took to make that happen, he would do.

Once inside the air-conditioned space, he fired up his laptop and started making calls on his phone. He needed answers and knew that the fastest way to get them was to check out social media. He had become friends on several of the local pages. As he had believed, the American love for posting what they saw, heard, thought, or believed online told him what he wanted to know.

This wasn't a big hit to the operation. It could be handled, with some small interventions at the right levels. An unstable man, high on meth, goes berserk on Main Street. That would be a good cover. It was sensational and yet believable. It was also not far from the truth. There would be a price to pay for this. He had to send a message to the rest of his men that this was not going to be tolerated. They had to stay focused on their jobs and, above all else, stay invisible.

His guest was coming to get an update on the operation. The man had been useful while setting up this operation but he had to be put in his place. He thought that his public standing afforded him a right to control how things were handled. He had to be made to understand that he wasn't in charge. He was only a tool to be used. He was still a useful tool, so he had to take care of him and handle him appropriately. A time was coming when his position and sources would no longer be necessary. He would then be discarded. Today was not that day, but it wasn't far away.

"How in the hell did this happen," the man demanded to know. "You said there wouldn't be any problems. You said there wouldn't be anything to worry about," he said, pacing back and forth. He was really worked up. His face was turning red.

Miguel enjoyed watching the man work himself up. When he talked the skin under his chin flopped around. It made Miguel think about the waddle on a turkey. He fought to control his smile.

"Well, guess what? I'm fucking worried." The man stopped and braced his hands on the table opposite Miguel. "I thought you had control over that group of fuck-ups!" he demanded. The man's voice had a plaintive note to it that wasn't present when he was talking to the press.

Miguel knew this man liked to be in control. He wasn't in control of this and was just beginning to realize how little control he had.

"Careful amigo, you wouldn't want someone to hear you? They might question your loyalties. You wouldn't want that would you?" he asked as he leveled his gaze on the agitated man.

The man glared at Miguel. He didn't like to be challenged. That hard look melted away under the cold stare that was locked on him. He could feel the cold blue eyes as they bored into his soul. They held no compassion, no warmth. They were dead eyes and until that gaze passed the man couldn't breathe.

"Come, sit down, have a drink. All this pacing and shouting will not change what has happened. It changes nothing." Miguel waved his hand dismissively. He picked up the bottle from the silver serving tray. It was such a contrast, the fine silver sitting on the beat-up scarred wood of the table. The man poured the liquor into the fine cut crystal tumbler, carefully measuring out precisely three fingers worth. Once the liquor was poured, he raised his eyes to the man who was still standing.

"I said sit down."

He didn't raise his voice. He didn't need to. His voice, like his eyes, held no compassion.

"You know," Miguel said once his guest was seated, "I have come to truly appreciate fine Scotch. Many of my countrymen only drink tequila."

He slid the tumbler across the table. "Now, don't get me wrong my friend, I like my tequila too, but a fine scotch, now, that is something else altogether. You see, tequila is like a scorpion. It comes right out and stares you in the eye. It says fuck you *esse* and then it stings your ass. It might kill you. It will make you sick. But you definitely will remember its bite. Now, take this fine Scotch, it has a bite as well," he said pointing at the tumbler. Condensation was forming on the side of the glass.

"The difference is that it starts out with a smooth burn that slowly engulfs all of you. It does not sting you," he said, shaking his head.

He quickly leaned forward, placing his hands on the side of the glass, the ropy muscles in his forearms flexing as he pressed his hands down on the table. "It consumes you. It consumes you, and you don't even realize it until it is too late."

"You see my friend that is what we have done here. We moved slowly. We took our time, set things up one step at a time. We are here. This is our town," he said, sweeping his arm in the general direction of the town. "This problem on Main Street is only a small bump in the road," he said as he dismissively waved his hand. "Yes, we will be careful, but we do not need to stop our operation."

"Drink up my friend and let the beast warm your heart," Miguel told him as he leaned back in his chair.

The Senator drank down the Scotch, but the chill from his friend's eyes tamped out the fire of the beast. In fact, he'd never felt so cold in his life. He knew that the man had spoken the truth. The beast had consumed him, and there was no going back again.

TL Scott grew up in a small mid-western town. He could often be found with his nose in a good book, even while walking around. Small town life was good, but he craved adventure. He wanted to make a difference with his life, so he joined the Navy. Over the course of his Naval career, Scott was exposed to people from all walks of life. It is from his love of storytelling and passion for characters of all types that give his characters life. They are the ones that tell their story.

Scott's break-out novel A Life Worth Living is a tale of a family's struggles with love and loss. Dave and Debbie have grown distant from each other while trying to juggle successful careers and two children. When tragedy strikes, they must decide how much they are willing to sacrifice to make theirs A Life Worth Living.

His second novel, Fault Line, follows Bill and his buddies. They are visiting his hometown while on leave from the war. Bill's baby sister is getting married. The soldiers are forced into action when they cross the path of a gang that has invaded this idyllic western town. There is no way this gang could have settled in so deep without help. Someone had to have helped them. Someone has crossed the line, the Fault Line.

His third book, Levels, was released in November of 2018. When you board an elevator, you do so as an act of faith. You have faith that when the doors open you will be where you intended to be. For Jake, that is not always the case.

Made in the USA
Lexington, KY
29 November 2019